The dream of Danni's life was to succeed in the male-orientated world of motor racing—until Shiloh O'Rourke came along and racing didn't seem so important any more. But then Danni found herself facing the question—if Shiloh had really been connected with her brother's death, shouldn't he be made to pay?

RACE FOR REVENGE

BY

LYNSEY STEVENS

MILLS & BOON LIMITED
15–16 BROOK'S MEWS
LONDON W1A 1DR

First published 1981
Australian copyright 1981
Philippine copyright 1981
This edition 1981

© Lynsey Stevens 1981

ISBN 0 263 73685 7

Set in Monophoto Baskerville 11 on 11½ pt.

Made and printed in Great Britain by
Richard Clay (The Chaucer Press) Ltd,
Bungay, Suffolk

CHAPTER ONE

The high-powered 1600c.c. engine roared like the thoroughbred it was as the driver accelerated down the straight, competent gloved hands firmly manipulating the small racing wheel. The speedometer flickered past one hundred and sixty kilometres per hour and the bitumen roadway flashed beneath the car like a movie on fast return. The driver's concentration remained fixed on the manipulation of the hurtling vehicle. With the approaching curve hands and feet moved with split-second precision on gears and brakes as the bright yellow Lola sped smoothly around the private practice track.

The driver completed another five laps before the car slowed, rolling to a halt on the asphalt apron in front of a large galvanised iron shed which was obviously, judging by the sophisticated tools and mechanical equipment housed therein, a garage and workshop worthy of a more than average amateur mechanic. One large toolbox lay open on the tarmac displaying concertina-like shelves of well used paraphernalia.

In the dim shadow of the shed a tall figure, clad in faded and ancient jeans and an equally faded and misshapen shirt of uncertain vintage, leant nonchalantly with a shoulder against one wall, watching the yellow car make its final lap and come to a stop. The lazy relaxed stance of that figure in no way indicated the almost catlike watchfulness of the eyes following every move of the racer as its driver put it through its paces. The face was long and thin, and it was pale and suntanned, as though its owner had recently suffered prolonged ill-health. Tawny yellow-brown eyes were screwed up to mere slits against the sun's glare despite the dark glasses perched on the straight nose.

A rather faded and frayed cap bearing an almost unreadable advertisement for a particular brand of motor oil was pulled over unruly fair hair which protruded from beneath the cap in tangled disorder, as though the wind had twisted it every which way.

However, the state of his hair, no more than the rest of his appearance, was of little importance to the watcher at that particular moment as he absently chewed a blade of grass between strong white teeth. For although his gaze followed intently the route of the yellow Formula Ford racing car, the harsh set of his expression and the pain in his eyes indicated that at least some part of his mind was fixed at another place, another time, and that his memories would have been better left as far from his present thoughts as was possible.

As the car came to a smooth halt in front of the shed the driver sprang agilely from the cramped cockpit, leaving the engine to idle in the warmth of the early afternoon sun. The man noticed absently that the driver was surprisingly short and the faded blue driving suit gave the appearance of stoutness. However, the suit was obviously several sizes too large, the sleeves being folded back under the driving gloves and the legs rolled neatly above stout driving boots.

The driver's back was to the shed and, unaware of the audience, gloved hands removed the bright red safety helmet and placed it in the cockpit, leaving the dark head-covering balaclava in place. The driver appeared to listen intently to the throbbing engine for some time before choosing a long-shafted screwdriver from the toolbox which had been left open from earlier use. The figure deftly removed the engine covering and leaned over the engine, making some slight adjustment that was unable to be seen by the onlooker. Then the driver stood back once more to listen, hands resting lightly on hips.

Only then did the other figure straighten from the shadows to throw the blade of grass to one side and walk slowly forward. A slight stiffness, almost a limp, marred the purposeful stride of the man and the noise of the high-powered engine successfully blanketed the sound of his footsteps.

'I'd say another half turn should do it.' His deep voice barely climbed above the throb of the engine, but it was loud enough to startle the other figure into spinning around, the screwdriver clattering to the asphalt from the gloved hand.

Blue eyes, round with alarm, had flown to the stranger's face and as he bent over to retrieve the tool the man was surprised at the youthfulness of the face almost covered by the dark balaclava. Under the startled blue gaze he leant over the racer, gave a slight twist of the screwdriver, cocked an ear to the timbre of the engine, and with a shrug of satisfaction reached across to switch off the ignition. The grassy paddock in which the practice track had been set out fell silent, although not for long.

By this time the driver had recovered sufficiently for outraged anger to replace the momentary alarm in the blue eyes. 'Just what do you think you're doing?' Anger had raised the pitch of the youth's voice to a feminine tone, causing the man to grin crookedly down at the boy.

'Giving you the benefit of my years of experience.'
White teeth flashed and two deep creases were
etched in either cheek beneath the black anonymity
of the sunglasses. The smile transformed the thin pale
face, although this fact was lost on the owner of the
car. 'You know, you handle the car pretty well for a
kid.'

'A kid! A kid?' The voice spluttered and rose still
higher, and if the stamping of one booted foot didn't
make it obvious to the tall man that regrettably he
had made a mistaken observation, then the cascade
of dark waving curls that tumbled out of the angrily
removed balaclava finally decided the issue.

The transformation was astounding. Shoulder-
length dark hair swung about an attractive face,
tanned and vitally healthy, with full bow-shaped lips
now firmly set in anger, a small upturned nose dusted
with light freckles and dark-fringed, almost violet-blue
eyes.

The girl drew herself up to her full height of around
five foot two, bringing the man's attention to a hint
of rounded curves beneath the enveloping driving
suit. 'Why, you ... you ...' Words seemed to fail the
girl, and still more colour rose to her cheeks.

This amused the stranger further and his broad
shoulders shook with suppressed mirth until he could
no longer contain it and he burst out laughing, his
eyes dancing in his thin face. The uncompromising
stance and still set expression of the girl sobered him
slightly and with amusement still written on his face
he shrugged his shoulders.

'I offer my apologies for my unfortunate mistake,
but you must admit that ninety-nine per cent of
motor racing drivers are men, so the odds were

stacked in my favour.'

'Do you realise you could have undone weeks of work with your ... your high-handed interference?' The girl's hands rested sternly on her hips and her chin was set aggressively. 'For your information, I'll be racing at Surfers next weekend and we've been preparing this car for weeks especially for that race. You could have ruined everything!' she finished, her eyes round and flashing.

'It did need an extra half turn,' he grinned.

'That's beside the point. How am I to know whether you know what you're doing or not? You could be anyone. I don't know you from Adam,' she raised her hands.

He removed his sunglasses and shoved them into the pocket on the short sleeve of his sweat-shirt. 'Allow me to introduce myself. Shiloh O'Rourke.' A slight wariness crossed his face as he swept off his disreputable cap and ran a hand over his fair hair in an attempt to restore it to some order.

The girl was struck by the unusual colour of his eyes. They were light brown, flecked with yellow, and tiger-bright, and as they looked straight into her own she felt her heartbeats quicken and a never before experienced trembling fluttered in the pit of her stomach. She blinked uncertainly, not understanding the sensations he seemed to have created within her, and her uncertainty rekindled her slightly wavering anger. Dark brows drew together.

'Shiloh? I don't believe it!' She clutched at a reason for her revived ire. 'What kind of a name is that supposed to be? No one's called Shiloh.'

'I am.' He didn't seem to have taken offence at her terse remarks. 'Shiloh David O'Rourke, to be precise. My mother is an American, a member of an

old Northern family, a number of whom have tradi-
tionally been named after famous battles or generals of
the American Civil War. Hence Shiloh. And a very
historical battle I was,' he continued. 'The Confeder-
ates played a long shot at the Battle of Shiloh, attack-
ing the Yankees with forty thousand men early one
Sunday morning, taking them completely by surprise. The Union won the battle by the skin of its
teeth and Shiloh was one of the bloodiest battles of
the war, accounting for about twenty thousand men
killed or wounded. A log chapel nearby, called
Shiloh Church, gave its name to the battle, and subsequently yours truly.'

The girl was looking at him sceptically.

'I suppose I can be thankful for small mercies. I
could have been stuck with Gettysburg or Bull Run,'
he grinned in that same crooked fashion, causing her
heart to skip in the most absurd manner. 'I've even
had a song written about me, or don't you dig Neil
Diamond?'

'I recall the song and, actually, I don't mind Neil
Diamond.' She raised her chin. 'I can take him or
leave him,' she added, thinking she might have
backed down.

'Most girls would probably take him.' The
amusement played around his mouth.

A very attractive mouth, she noticed, and frown-
ingly pulled herself up on the thought.

'And to whom have I made myself known?' he
asked, grinning winningly down at her from his lofty
six-foot-one-inch height. Had the girl but known it,
that particular smile, part and parcel of his unconscious charm, had won him more than his share of
attention from members of the fair sex of his
acquaintance, and this girl was not unaware of the

magnetic quality of that smile.

She had to admit that he was attractive in an untidy, devil-may-care kind of way. She wondered offhandedly how old he was. It was hard to pinpoint his age. His face bore signs of experience and yet his engaging grin took years off the thinness of his features. She guessed at anything between twenty-five and thirty-five.

In her moments of hesitation he watched the play of emotions across her face before she made her decision and reluctantly replied, 'Danielle Mathieson.'

He was obviously a little taken aback.

'You're Danni?' he asked incredulously.

She nodded coolly. 'My friends,' she emphasised, 'call me Danni.' And although she hadn't added, 'You can call me Miss Mathieson,' she felt the unspoken words hanging in the air space between them and experienced a moment of contrition at her rudeness.

However, her sarcasm seemed to make little or no impression on him. 'When Rick spoke of his kid sister Danni, I somehow got the impression that you were about ten or twelve.'

'I'm twenty-two,' replied Danni with dignity, and then her expression softened, adding a certain wistfulness to her piquant face. 'You . . . you knew Rick?'

Shiloh O'Rourke was not unmoved by the sadness in her face and he nodded, setting his fair hair quivering into windblown disorder. 'We raced together and he was a friend,' he said simply, a distant look tinged with a certain cautiousness in his cat's eyes, and there was a cynical twist to his mouth.

Danni felt tears spring to her eyes as a dozen questions formed in her mind, but the lump in her throat which she tried valiantly to swallow prevented any of them from being voiced.

Shiloh ran his hand over his eyes and down his cheek, shaking his thoughts back to the present. 'I can't understand how our paths have failed to cross before now. I know you followed Rick's career, but I'm sure I haven't seen you at the track.'

'No, you probably wouldn't have. I never travelled the circuits with Rick. I only ever saw him race up here at Surfers and once or twice at Lakeside. I was still at school when he started competing seriously, when he joined Chris Damien's team, and I—well, I promised my father I'd stick with my studies until the end of my course.' She paused slightly. 'I was on a camping holiday in England when . . . when Rick was killed. By the time word had caught up with me I couldn't make it back home in time for the funeral. Did you . . . were you there the day of that race at Sandown?'

The man paused before answering, that same air of wariness in his eyes. 'Yes,' he replied at last. 'Yes, I was there.' What could only be described as a flinch of pain fleetingly crossed his face and his expression was momentarily bleak and almost vulnerable. He went to add more, but changed his mind, his lips closing firmly, tension in the lines around his mouth.

'Would you like to come up to the house?' she asked hesitantly. 'My father won't be home until later, but I'm sure he'd like to see you if you're a friend of Rick's.'

Shiloh O'Rourke looked down at his disreputable attire and grimaced ruefully. 'Well, I'm not exactly dressed for visiting. I was taking a burn on a motorcycle I've just overhauled, testing it out, and at the same time clearing the cobwebs, when I noticed the sign on the gate, Mallaroo Stud. Rick often spoke about your horse Stud out this way and that, coupled with the sight of the yellow Formula Ford racing around the track, was enough to bring me inside. I'm afraid my curiosity got the better of me.'

For the first time Danni noticed the motorcycle, a battered safety helmet balanced on the seat, parked alongside her little red Gemini sedan in the shade of the shed.

'Don't worry about your clothes. As I said, any friend of Rick's is welcome at our place.' She noticed his eyes flinched from her and frowned slightly, wondering what she could have said to upset him. 'At any rate,' she hurried on, 'we don't judge on appearances and neither of us are strangers to a bit of oil and grease.' Danni laughed. 'Rick used to say that I was really a blonde but that I'd had my head stuck in so many engines with him that the grease had rubbed off, making me a brunette!'

Shiloh laughed, and this time the humour reached his eyes as they turned to Danni's dark hair as it shone in the sunlight.

Danni herself was unable to prevent her gaze from moving over Shiloh's tall figure, over the faded cap, unruly hair and thin, smiling face, the faded jeans and shirt and the long well-worn cyclists' boots. At the moment he couldn't be called well dressed, but he wasn't unclean. And the old clothes couldn't hide the breadth of his shoulders and the strong muscular strength he seemed to exude.

At least part of her thoughts must have been reflected in her face, for the object of her close scrutiny was grinning at her again in that tolerantly amused way he had about him, making her feel all of twelve years old at the very most.

Frowning at him, she turned back to the racer. 'I'll just put the car away,' she said tersely.

'I'll do that for you,' he said goodhumouredly, and she had to stand back in exasperation while he effortlessly pushed the car into the shed, packed up the toolbox and returned it to its place and finally secured the lock on the shed door.

'What do you do when you're not racing Formula Fords? Just muck about the farm?' he asked innocently.

'I'm an assistant librarian at the Gold Coast City Council Library at Burleigh Heads,' she replied, fuming inwardly, 'so I only have weekends free for racing. And I enjoy library work as well,' she added firmly.

He nodded without noticing her annoyance. 'And how long have you been racing?' he asked as they walked across to where Danni's car and his bike were parked.

'About a year, although the race next weekend— that's Round One of the Driver to Europe Competition—will be the first really serious bit of competitive driving I've done,' she told him.

'Mmm. I'm not generally in favour of women mixing it with men in motor racing, but I guess you must have met the requirements to have your nomination accepted in the series,' he remarked loftily.

'What do you mean "mixing it with men"?' Danni's hackles rose. He really was too much! 'There's no reasonable reason why women shouldn't be able to compete in motor racing if they're competent enough. I've never heard anything so narrow-minded in my life!' Two pink spots of colour tinged her cheeks as she warmed to her argument. 'I suppose you think a woman's place is in the home, running after you, feeding you, doing your washing and ironing?'

Shiloh's grin infuriated her more. 'Well, there would be certain compensations,' he said wickedly, and Danni flushed.

'I'll have you know, Shiloh O'Rourke,' she said angrily, not wanting to dwell on his outrageous statement, 'that I am a very competent driver, and when I'm racing I neither ask for nor give any quarter.'

Shiloh held up a hand. 'Okay, Danni.' He picked up his safety helmet and shoved his cap into the pocket of his jeans. 'One thing Rick failed to mention was that his sister was something of a virago,' he grinned.

'I'm sorry,' she found herself smiling back, 'but that subject's something of a "pass me my soapbox" to me. Are you coming up to the house?' she asked.

Once again she caught that wariness about him.

'No, I won't come up to the house today, Danni. Maybe another time.' His eyes moved over her slight figure. 'I'll amend that to definitely another time.' He grinned at the disconcerted flush on her face. 'My parents have invited people over this evening for dinner and I promised to put in an appearance—suitably attired, of course. Do you think I should change my jeans?' he asked, and they both laughed.

Danni stood by her car watching his motorcycle as it moved down the track to the gate of their property and then picked up speed on the road heading back towards the Gold Coast. She climbed slowly into the car and backed it around in the opposite direction.

Shiloh O'Rourke? she thought as she drove towards the sprawling ranch-style house that was just over a kilometre from the entrance gate. There was something about him that worried her. Well, perhaps worried was a little too strong a description, but . . . She couldn't put her finger on exactly what it was. At times she had felt he was watching her, gauging her reactions, carefully choosing his words when answering her questions.

It was strange that she couldn't remember Rick ever mentioning him. Shiloh O'Rourke. It was such an unusual name she surely would have remembered it had she heard it before. And he'd spoken of Rick as though they had known each other well. He'd also said he was at the race meeting on the day Rick had lost his life driving his Formula 5000.

Shiloh O'Rourke. O'Rourke. A tiny niggling memory nudged her mind and floated away before she could take hold of it. There was something there that refused to come to the surface. Oh, well, if she didn't force it it would return in time, she reflected as she garaged her car and ran up the wide low steps on to the covered patio that ran the length of the house.

She'd have a refreshing shower and then decide what to prepare for her father for dinner. As she opened the screen door the phone rang and she walked into the hall to pick up the receiver.

'Danni? Dallas here,' said a familiar voice.

'Dallas, what's the trouble? Is Pop all right?' Danni's heart jerked painfully. Since Rick's death over a year ago her father had seemed to grow into an old man in no time.

'No trouble, Danni,' chuckled Dallas, sounding most unlike his usual sober self. 'Your father and I met up with some friends of his at the R.S.L. Club and we decided we'd had a few too many drinks to drive to Mallaroo tonight. We're going to stay here in town and head off in the morning. We'll probably pass you on your way in.'

'Oh. Well, make sure you both have a good meal tonight,' said Danni, relieved that her father was not ill.

'Will do. How did the car go today?' asked Dallas, who was an exceptionally good mechanic and, with Danni, made up the sum total of her racing team.

'Like a dream, as always,' replied Danni. 'You're a wonder, Dallas, and I'm lucky to have you on my side.'

'That's what I keep telling you, Danni. If I say it often enough you're going to start believing me,' he laughed again.

Dallas Byrne was a tall and pleasant-looking young man, with fierce red hair, a drooping moustache, also red, and blue eyes in a fair freckled face. Had he been dark and swarthy Danni always thought he would have looked more like a Mexican bandit than a Mexican bandit looked. He was twenty-five and had owned and raced his own cars. However, although his cars had been mechanically first class, he admitted himself that he had been only a mediocre driver and often laughingly said he lacked the killer instinct to take him to the front.

It was a pity, Danni mused as she rang off, that Dallas needed a couple of drinks to allow him to relax his usual staid personality. She had known him for some time, often met him socially, and when she purchased her Formula Ford he had offered his services as mechanic. His skill was well known and Danni was pleased to have him as he kept her car in perfect condition, teaching her even more about auto-mechanics than Rick had.

He had asked her out with undaunted regularity and on the odd occasion that she had agreed to go she had always enjoyed his company. He accepted her restrictions that they keep their relationship on a purely friendly basis, but he made her aware of the fact that he lived in hope of her having a change of heart.

Because Dallas made no more demands than she was prepared to fulfil Danni had grown quite fond of him and a lot of their friends accepted them as a going couple. Occasionally she had wished she could allow herself to become involved with him as he was such a calm and dependable person, but ... Her instincts told her he was far too nice to be taken advantage of and Danni suspected that the idea of her driving the Formula Ford had a considerable amount to do with his admiration.

Maybe Dallas would know something about Shiloh O'Rourke. She should have asked him while he was on the phone. Dallas knew or knew of everyone even vaguely connected with the motor racing scene. She wished she could remember herself. It was so frustrating.

Shiloh's face, not handsome, but somehow arresting, came vividly to mind. His remembered attractiveness caused her to catch her breath. She knew she was attracted to him physically, but at the same time, she told herself, there was something about him that irritated her, sparked her usually even temper. He was definitely arrogant, for all the teasing goodnatured impression he seemed to exude.

And he had treated her like a teenager barely out of the schoolroom. Her lips set sternly ... He had at first mistaken her for a youth, and yet his eyes told her that he was aware of her attractions, made it very plain, in fact. A tingling sensation moved up her spinal column, as though his fingertips had moved over her body.

Giving herself a mental shake, she strode irritably through the hall to her bedroom. Here there was peacefulness. The tonings were all restful, subdued pastel-shaded wallpaper and complementary deep-pile carpet. Her bedroom suite was painted white and the single bed was covered by an eggshell blue chenille quilt.

The only vibrant part of the room was a framed poster-sized colour photograph hanging on the wall. It was a shot Danni had taken herself of her brother, Rick, when he'd won a major race at Surfers Paradise International Speedway about three years earlier. He was sitting on the back of the cockpit of his bright red Formula 5000; a colourful lei of flowers had been placed around his neck and a frothing bottle of champagne was clasped in his raised hand. His dark hair was lifting in the breeze and his face was alight with the delighted smile of the victor. In fact, the glow of victory and the exhilaration of the race shone in his dark eyes. The photograph had so much life that Danni had to swallow the lump that rose in her throat.

She turned away, taking a fresh set of underclothes from her drawer, her gaze falling on another smaller framed photograph standing on the top of her dressing table. It was a family study of Pop and herself with Rick, before he had started on his motor racing career professionally.

Danni walked across to the open window of her bedroom and stood gazing out over the tree-covered hills, her eyes not seeing their rural beauty, caught in the distress of bittersweet memories. Sighing, she collected her towelling bathrobe and made her way slowly to the bathroom. Under the shower, the cool jets of spray playing over her young body, she found her thoughts returning to Shiloh O'Rourke and his possible association with Rick. Perhaps Shiloh could fill her in on the details of that fateful day; he said he had been there.

For some time now she had been trying to find a way to broach the subject of that race with her father, but he still seemed loath to talk about it. And she respected that. She knew just how close her father and her brother had been, and she didn't want to add to her father's pain. She had sounded Dallas out about it one day, but he had been embarrassed, and besides, he hadn't been at Sandown the day of Rick's death.

On her return from London the race, Rick's death, the funeral and the enquiry had been over and no one had given Danni anything but the barest details. Up until recently she hadn't wanted to know. It was painful enough to grow accustomed to the fact that they would never see Rick again.

A multitude of unbidden feelings passed through her mind and she had to admit that lately she had felt almost shut out for the first time in her life. Shut out of the family tragedy, and the feeling was not a comforting one, no matter that her father wanted to save her any unhappiness.

Rick had always treated her as an equal, always had time for the little sister who had tagged along after him, asking interminable questions, listening to his answers with bright adoring eyes. Her brother had shared his thoughts with her, his aspirations, his feelings about everything. And yet he had never once mentioned this Shiloh O'Rourke. Not that she could remember. And that was strange.

But then why should he have mentioned everyone he met to her? asked a small voice inside her. Rick wasn't bound to tell her everything. She had no longer been his little sister and he—well, he had no longer been the confidant of her teens.

In the half dozen or so years before his death he had taken on other interests and responsibilities, among them a career in motor racing, a very promising career that had been cut short when Danni had been across the other side of the world. But perhaps she should admit, if she were honest, that she had lost that special part of her brother years before the crashing of his Formula 5000 had taken his life.

Tears rolled down her cheeks to be lost in the shower spray. It was months since she had allowed herself to cry over her brother's death. She had had to remain calm and in command of herself for Pop's sake, and now here she was weeping like a baby. And the catalyst was that Shiloh O'Rourke. Her heart felt bruised and a wave of self-pity washed over her.

Determinedly she shook it off, depression giving way to anger directed firstly at herself and then at the attractive fair-haired face that swam before her.

'Damn Shiloh O'Rourke!' she said forcefully at the shower spray, then smiled shakily at the ridiculousness of her outburst.

She could hardly, in all fairness, blame him, she thought, stepping resolutely from the shower. She began to towel herself dry on a fluffy blue bath sheet. The dam had been building up inside her for ages and if it hadn't been the appearance of Shiloh O'Rourke it would have been someone or something else that set off the crack in the wall of emotional restraint she had built up.

But she couldn't help feeling a lingering unease, that there was something important she hadn't been told. She felt it from the very beginning, from her arrival back in Australia, and Shiloh O'Rourke had only added to that feeling. The urge to know more about the whole thing began to grow within her and she knew now that she wouldn't rest until she had heard the full story.

And Shiloh O'Rourke would be the most logical person to tackle about it. Her father had suffered enough and she knew in all probability he would only tell her a part of the story, glossing over anything he thought might distress her.

If only she'd been here at the time, instead of touring England, then she could have known the proper progression of events, read the newspaper reports. Her eyes flew open. Of course, she could go to the library and look up the back issues of the newspapers. As a library assistant she should have known that this was the obvious thing to do. She would go along to the Southport Library as soon as she could manage it and maybe then she would be in full possession of the facts. And there would be no need to cause her father any distress by mentioning the painful subject.

CHAPTER TWO

NEXT morning Danni did think she might have found time to visit the main library at Southport before she started work in the branch at Burleigh Heads. However, things didn't work out that way. By the time she had done a little housework at Mallaroo and then driven down to their house in Broadbeach, where she stayed during the week while she was working, her plans to delve into the back issues of the newspapers had had to be shelved.

Besides, it had crossed her mind all of a sudden that perhaps she wouldn't want to know all the details of that day. Maybe it would be as well to let it all remain quietly in the past.

Now she had parked her car in the library car park and with a little less than half an hour before she was due to start work she decided to walk across to the shopping centre and relax over a cup of coffee in her favourite coffee shop.

'Hi, Danni! Danni!' A voice filtered slowly through her thoughts as she drained her coffee cup. A pretty young fair-haired girl slid into the seat opposite Danni, her face alight with the glow of someone bearing good tidings.

'Oh, hello, Lisa,' replied Danni vaguely, dragging her thoughts back from yesterday's encounter on the practice track. 'Sorry I didn't hear you at first, I was thinking about something or other.'

'By the look on your face you were miles away,' said Lisa. 'What deep dark thoughts were you thinking?'

'Nothing important,' said Danni quickly, not wanting to discuss Shiloh O'Rourke with anyone, let alone Lisa, who was an inveterate gossip.

Her workmate was four years younger than Danni and she was the junior assistant at the library. Lisa was a pretty girl and Danni liked her very much. They worked well together, although their natures and interests were so very different. Outside of her job Lisa's main pursuits were pop music and young men. Her practically non-stop chatter about the latter, of which she seemed to have a never-ending stream, sometimes made Danni feel as old as Methuselah.

However, Danni was unaware that the younger girl's opinion of her bordered very nearly on hero-worship. Lisa admired Danni's poise, the quiet friendly manner which seemed to draw people of all ages to her, and the enjoyment Danni found in talking to everyone who crossed her path.

The fact that Danni went out at the weekend among a group of men and raced her car against them, mingled with them after the race meetings, knew them all by name and spoke to them on equal terms never failed to impress the younger girl. That only on very rare occasions did any of these young men present themselves at the library to see Danni was always a source of incomprehension and disbelief as Lisa saw it. She knew Danni seldom went out on dates and if she did accept an invitation from one of these young men he was rarely around for more than a few weeks. On the odd occasion that Lisa had tentatively questioned Danni about what she called Danni's 'love life', the older girl had simply laughed and said she wasn't ready to settle down to anything steady and wouldn't be for years yet.

Lisa often sighed over the problem. As far as she

was concerned Danni was very nearly an old maid, ready to gather dust on the shelf marked 'Romance' and, in her opinion, it was a wicked waste. Danni was so attractive and what was more, she was a darned nice girl.

'What brings you over all agog?' asked Danni.

'I saw you walk across here earlier and I knew you'd be having a cup of coffee before work, so I raced over in my morning tea break so I could tell you right away about this gorgeous guy who came into the library this morning.' Lisa's voice was alive with excitement. 'And he was looking for you!' She played her trump card.

'Someone asked especially for me?' Danni frowned, a niggling flash of a thin face topped with untidy hair slid to the front of her mind and her heart began to behave peculiarly. She tried to still the tremble of her lips and quickly raised her empty coffee cup to her mouth in case Lisa should notice.

'Yes.' Lisa was beaming. 'And he was fantastic, really spunky. Tall and fair. You know how I adore blonds?' she giggled. 'He had a lovely smile and was really well-mannered. Where have you been hiding him, Danni?'

'Did he say who he was?' Danni asked, all sorts of emotions tossing about inside her. Maybe it was someone with a message about next weekend's race meeting? But no, they would probably phone her if there were any changes there.

'No, he didn't say. He just walked up to the counter and smiled at me. Gosh, my legs turned to water! Then he said, "Would Miss Danni Mathieson be here?"' Lisa sighed. 'I was planning to turn my charm on him when I noticed him walking in, but after he mentioned your name—well, I never try to cut out a friend, Danni, you know that. It's one of my steadfast rules.'

Danni suppressed a smile at Lisa's expression. 'I don't suppose he said what he wanted, did he?'

'No.' Lisa shook her head. 'I tried to worm it out of him, but he just smiled away until I couldn't think straight.' She frowned in concentration. 'Let's see now. When I said you wouldn't be in until ten-thirty—this was about nine o'clock—he said that was a pity and he looked quite disappointed. He said he'd hoped to catch you this morning as he was going up to Brisbane on business for a few days and wouldn't have time to telephone you. Then he asked me what times you were working on Thursday, and when I said you'd be in all day until five o'clock he said he'd call back then. Wow, he's a dish, Danni! He thanked me and, as he went to walk away, I asked him who should I tell Danni had been asking for her. That was quick thinking, wasn't it? And do you know what he said?'

Danni shook her head, the picture of Shiloh O'Rourke not fading in the slightest, but seeming to grow brighter every minute.

'He grinned and said that if I told you he was sure as eggs you'd find an excuse not to be here. He said he'd keep you guessing. What a sense of humour! Then he left.' Lisa's eyes were round. 'Have you any ideas about who he could be, Danni?'

'I don't suppose he had untidy hair and wore ancient jeans, did he?' Danni asked drily.

'Well, not exactly untidy, but sort of wavy,' replied Lisa. 'You mean you do know who he is?' When the other girl shrugged her shoulders expressionlessly she continued, 'His jeans looked brand new. Dark blue bogarts, I think. Oh, and he had on a T-shirt with something written on the front of it. Now, what was it? Some place I'd never heard of. Brand something. Brands Hatch—that was it. Does that mean anything to you? Have you worked out who it is?'

Danni shrugged her shoulders again. 'Could be anyone,' she said matter-of-factly. 'Brands Hatch is a racing circuit in England.'

'Oh, Danni, what a mystery! Could he be a racing driver? It might be someone who's worshipped you from afar. I can hardly wait till Thursday, can you?' Lisa beamed.

'Oh, yes! I can hardly wait,' replied Danni expressively.

'I've got a feeling about this, Danni. I think he's really taken with you.' Lisa's eyes shone with the romance of it all.

'So have I got a feeling,' said Danni, standing up, 'a feeling we'd better get going or we'll be late.'

On Thursday morning Danni was suffering from a mixture of anticipation and apprehension. For reasons she refused to analyse part of her, a part she was finding hard to quell, was excitedly looking forward to seeing Shiloh O'Rourke again, while she had to keep reminding herself that he had been arrogant and high-handed as well as making it obvious that he didn't like women on the track.

And that was Danni's bugbear. She'd had to fight to gain every inch of the respect she now had in the motor racing fraternity and her one aim was to take out the Driver to Europe series, to be the first woman to do so.

This turmoil inside her found an outlet in causing her to drop just about everything she had picked up, including a carton of milk that morning and a large

stack of non-fiction books she had sorted ready for
re-shelving just five minutes ago.

All this was a source of great amusement for Lisa,
who admitted that she was almost as excited as
Danni refused to admit she was. Danni hoped fervently that if Shiloh did arrive at the library he would
do so while Lisa was on her lunch break. To have
the beaming Lisa as an audience would really top
the occasion off nicely.

Shiloh's reason for calling to see her had Danni
baffled. Mulling over that reason for the past two
days, she had decided it could only have something
to do with motor racing. Surely it couldn't be that
he was attracted to her? She hoped ardently that he
wasn't, although she felt a little disquieted when she
recalled the admiring glances he had given her that
afternoon at the practice track. Somehow she had a
feeling deep down that her rather ordered world
might never be quite the same again if she allowed
him to come too close. If Lisa was right ... She
pulled herself up short. She was becoming as fanciful
as the other girl. Why would Shiloh O'Rourke be
interested in her, after the way she had treated him,
too? But she had been provoked.

Not that she had any desire to get to know him
anyway, she told herself. It was laughable. She could
barely stand him. He just wasn't her type. Of course,
she could refuse to see him, but she would like to
talk to him about Rick if she could. But that was all.

So why, she asked herself, was she fluttering about
like a bemused shrinking violet waiting for the man
of her dreams to suggest an assignation? She smiled
to herself at her flowery expressions. That was what
came of reading too many historical romances!

Danni glanced at the clock. It was just past

midday, so she collected her salad roll and apple and the novel she was currently reading and informed the other girls that she would be out for her lunch hour.

'Oh, Danni, you can't leave the library. What if your mystery man calls while you're away?' asked Lisa, most upset, and thinking that Danni was throwing away her biggest chance. 'I told you I had a feeling about him, and it's growing stronger. It really is.'

Danni wrinkled her nose. 'I'll only be across the road under my favourite tree,' she replied. 'Should he turn up, which he probably won't, you can have the honour of sending him right on over, Lisa. If, as you say, it's all meant to be, he'll be ready to climb mountains, swim raging torrents, etc., etc., to get to me, so crossing one minor road will be child's play for him.' She laughed as she headed out of the staff entrance.

Still smiling, she settled herself on a low bench in the shade of a spreading Moreton Bay fig tree. It was a wonderful day. The sky was Australian blue and the surf off to the left was pure turquoise and inviting. A cool fresh breeze moved the pine tree branches and brought the tang of the crystal sand and salty ocean across to her as she sat eating her lunch, engrossed in her novel.

At least, to all outward appearances she was engrossed in her book. Only Danni knew that her eyes flittered over the page without taking in a word of the story. She could imagine Lisa glancing out of the library and remarking to the librarian that Danni was a cool one, sitting placidly reading a book while she, Lisa, in the same position, would have been simply paralytic with nervousness and the waiting.

By the time Danni had finished her lunch she was exasperated with herself. She had wasted half of her lunch hour lifting her eyes to follow every motor-cycle that passed within hearing distance and studying everyone who looked remotely as if they were about to enter the library opposite. Last night she had been absorbed in this very book and when her drooping eyelids had forced her to set it aside she could hardly wait to get back to it. Now she was hard pressed to recall the plot.

Firmly she put Shiloh O'Rourke from her mind and concentrated on her story, the heroine of which was an independent miss who was under the impression that she wanted nothing more than to elope with a poverty-stricken and totally unsuitable young gentleman. Danni became caught up in a lengthy description of a visit to Vauxhall Gardens from where the heroine planned to make her escape, and she was oblivious of the fact that a tall thin figure was making his way across the road towards her until she became aware of a pair of familiar dusty well-worn motor-cyclist's boots entering the line of her vision.

Her eyes moved up the jean-clad legs, the dark blue denim hugging his muscular thighs like a second skin. His belt buckle featured a chequered flag emblem and he wore a plain white shirt with a short denim jacket which matched his jeans. Apart from his dusty boots he looked reasonably respectable, although he hadn't bothered to fasten the press studs on the cuffs of his jacket.

He was bare-headed now, but Danni could see by the dampened flattened fair hair that he had been wearing a crash helmet, and as the wind was beginning to lift his hair, drying its dampness, as each moment passed it started to wave into the abandoned disorder she remembered. He was smiling that particularly attractive smile which she seemed to have etched in her mind's eye and when he ran his hand through his tossled hair, enjoying the cooling effect of the breeze, her pulses began to race with gay abandon.

'Hi, Danni!' His deep voice caused her throat to constrict and she swallowed nervously. 'I noticed you sitting here when I pulled up. Nice place to spend your lunch hour. May I join you?' He sat down without waiting for her reply and unwrapped two cold cans of soft drink from a newspaper-wrapped parcel he was carrying. 'Whew, it's hot! I'm nearly parched with thirst. Which would you prefer, club lemon or Coke?' He crushed the wrapping into a ball and lobbed it neatly into an open garbage can some six feet away.

Danni tossed up as to whether or not she would refuse his offer on principle, but as he said, it was hot. And she was thirsty. 'Lemon, please.'

He ripped off the pull top and reaching into an inner pocket took out a straw which he stuck into her can before passing it to her. It crossed her mind that he hadn't even asked her if she wanted to use a straw and her lips tightened. He was being very solicitous, but the independent part of her personality jibed at his thoughtfulness. Perhaps the reason for this independence was the attitude of her father and her brother. To them she had always been equal. Equal opportunity and equal effort.

'I guess your young friend in the library told you I called in to see you on Monday,' Shiloh said easily, smiling at her as he folded the cuffs of his jacket neatly back from his wrists.

'Yes, I thought it must have been you,' Danni replied, catching sight of Lisa hanging out of the library window waving gaily. Lisa rarely missed anything and obviously she had recognised Danni's companion.

'So you knew it was me?' he grinned. 'Mental telepathy or a cultivated guess?'

Danni involuntarily looked pointedly at his hair and his grin widened. He ran a smoothing hand over his hair, not making much impression on its waving disorder.

'Something tells me you disapprove of my hair-style, Danni Mathieson. You know, I can't do a thing with it. It's a real cross for me to bear.' There was amusement in his tone. 'I must get it cut properly. I spent some time,' he paused almost imperceptibly, 'out of the swing of things and my last hairdresser was hardly a professional. If it's any consolation you aren't alone in your opinion. My mother says it offends her sensitivities and my father visibly blanches every time he turns my way. Guess you'll just have to love me for my sparkling personality.'

He held up his hand as Danni's back stiffened and her lips pursed. 'Sorry, just joking.' He took another drink from his can, his eyes dancing at her over the top. 'How long have you been working at the library?' He stepped over on to safer conversational grounds.

'Eight months here at Burleigh Heads. Nearly two years in all,' she replied coolly. 'I was working in the Coolangatta branch before I went to England for a few months to visit an aunt, my mother's sister. I went on a camping holiday there with my English cousins. Then,' she paused, 'then I came home and was lucky enough to get my old position back.'

Shiloh nodded, his face bearing that same cultivated and controlled expressionlessness. Although
Rick's death, the reason for Danni's return to Australia, hung in the air between them like something
tangible, neither made any mention of it, as though
they felt that it would drive a wedge between them.
They lapsed into silence, both studying their cans of
drink as though the words printed on them were
unfamiliar to them.

'I'll have to be getting back to work.' Danni
glanced at her watch. 'It's five to one.' She stood up
and smoothed the wrinkles from her rust-coloured
skirt.

Shiloh moved slowly to his feet, and as he made
to follow her across the road she noticed for the first
time that he favoured his right leg slightly, giving a
faint limp to his long stride.

Danni stepped off the pavement, only to have her
arm grabbed in a vice-like grip and she was jerked
back forcibly against his rock hard chest. Her hand
went out to save herself and her fingers encountered
the soft material of his body shirt.

'What the . . .?' she began, her eyes flashing angrily
to his face as a high-powered car streaked by, the
driver giving a warning blast on his horn. 'Oh!'
Danni expelled a breath and found it difficult to
draw another. Anger gave way to fright and relief
and her eyes grew large in her face. All at once she
noticed the nerve throbbing in Shiloh's tightly set
jaw and almost clinically she saw that his own face
had paled slightly. Beneath her hand she could feel
the steady thump of his heart as its beat accelerated
to match the race of her own. Danni's voice completely deserted her.

Shiloh shook his head in exasperation, breaking

the spark of awareness that flowed between them. 'Danni Mathieson, would you mind not throwing yourself under a car before I get to take you out to dinner?' He kept hold of her arm until they had safely negotiated the road and were standing in the parking area alongside his motorcycle.

'I . . . it's almost one. I'll have to go in. Thanks for the drink and,' she couldn't bring herself to look directly at him, her heightened awareness of him still flowing through her body, 'for—er—for preventing me from walking in front of that car.' She took a slow step towards the library, but his hand on her arm detained her. She looked down at that strong hand, wondering why the mere touch of those firm capable fingers could cause her senses to tense with responsiveness.

'Just a minute, Danni. You finish at five o'clock, don't you? Have dinner with me this evening?' For once his face was quite serious, or as serious as his smiling mouth could allow him to be.

Danni hesitated, searching her mind for an excuse. She could say she had to wash her hair.

As if he read her mind his eyes went to her hair and he grinned. 'No, your hair doesn't need washing, it looks very attractive as it is. You can write letters or do your ironing tomorrow night or next week. I'll give you until seven-thirty to get ready. How about it?' He smiled into her startled eyes with a devastating effect on her decision to firmly refuse his offer. 'Be a devil, Danni. Do something on impulse. I know a little restaurant that a friend of mine has recently taken over. The food's divine and I promise I'll try to be scintillating company.'

Danni wanted to say yes while part of her demanded she refuse him outright. Did she want to get involved with him? Should she follow her head or her heart?

'I'll even try to restrain my hair,' he said winningly.

A faint dimple appeared in Danni's cheek and she found herself smiling back at him, taking even herself by surprise. 'Well, all right.'

He grinned happily and touched her cheek with one finger. 'Great! I'll see you at seven-thirty, then.' He turned back to his bike and went to put on his skid-lid after getting her address from her.

'Shiloh!' Danni called him, and he stopped as he was about to swing his leg over the bike. 'What do I wear? Is it a dress-up place?'

'No—informal. Just wear something sexy.' Although only his eyes were visible behind the safety helmet his outrageous wink made her smile again. Maybe he wasn't so bad after all. At least he had a sense of humour. Besides, she could ask him about Rick tonight while they were having dinner.

He had kicked the starter and the engine fired. Lifting one hand in farewell, he turned out of the parking area and disappeared along the highway, leaving Danni to return to work to face the ecstatic Lisa.

By seven o'clock Danni had showered and changed ready for her evening out. All afternoon at work she had been plagued with questions by the excited Lisa. Who was the mystery man? What had he wanted? Did Danni know him? He was so handsome, didn't Danni think so? Was she going out with him?

Eventually Danni could stand the inquisition no longer and had put Lisa, and herself, out of their respective miseries. Thus Lisa's curiosity had been fed and Danni had been able to get on with her work without interruptions. Not that she had told Lisa all that much. After all, what was there to tell? Shiloh O'Rourke was an acquaintance with whom she was sharing a friendly dinner. There was no big deal, was there? Then why were her thoughts drifting continually back to the man?

She wore a cool pale blue sleeveless dress which was one of her favourites. The soft crêpe material hugged her figure while its thin straps left her nicely tanned shoulders bare. Her dark hair, shining with vitality and good health, swung about her face and she had used the minimum of make-up. She had only shaded her naturally pink lips with pearly lipstick and added a little mascara to her long curling lashes.

As she was touching her wrist with Tabu perfume a thought struck her without warning. How on earth was she going to ride pillion on Shiloh's motorcycle in this outfit? Apart from it being unsafe to ride a motorcycle with arms and legs bare, by the time they reached the restaurant she would be looking as though she had been dragged through a bush backwards.

Why hadn't she thought to ask him if he owned a car? And what was more to the point, why had she agreed to go out with him in the first place? She hadn't been able to stand the man when she first met him, she exaggerated. And her first impressions were usually quite sound.

She glanced at her wristwatch. He would be here in ten minutes. She might have time to change into a slack suit before he arrived. In a moment she had a pair of lightweight yellow slacks and matching jerkin out of her wardrobe and her hand was on the zipper of her dress when the doorbell chimed.

It could only be Shiloh. Drat the man! Danni moved out of her room to open the door, thinking he would just have to wait while she changed.

The light from the foyer fell on the figure standing on the landing, half turned to one side as he waited for her to answer his ring. As Danni opened the door he turned towards her and, for a split second, she didn't recognise him. Then he smiled and she felt his eyes travel appreciatively over her, over the pale blue dress that flared from the waist, a full lace-edged frill around the bottom of the skirt which swirled about her legs as she walked.

If his eyes moved over her, so she was staring at him in disbelief. He had had his hair cut and it was combed tidily in place, the back styled neatly above his collar. His pale blue, almost white shirt was open at the neck to halfway to his waist, the light reflecting from the surface of the gleaming medallion he wore around his neck, the medallion resting in the golden mat of fair hair on his chest. His shirt front was ruffled while the sleeves were a little fuller than normal and gathered to the wide cuffs.

He wore slacks of rich dark blue, fitting close to his thighs, and flaring from the knees, making him look even taller than ever. His shoes looked expensive and were polished to perfection and his whole outfit completely robbed Danni of speech. If he had added a black eye patch, a golden earring and a flashing cutlass he would have graced the deck of any pirate ship.

Taking his hand from behind his back, he presented her with a small corsage of Cooktown orchids, the smiling flash of his white teeth added further to his piratical good looks.

'They're beautiful. Thank you very much,' Danni stammered, taking the flowers from him, her face flushing hotly.

'They'll match your dress, too. Need some help to pin them on?' He stepped through the doorway.

Her slack suit forgotten, Danni carefully removed the delicate flowers, emblem of the state of Queensland, from their box and clipped them in place at the base of one of her shoulder straps. The delicate mauve shade of the flowers blended with the pale blue of her dress.

Shiloh nodded appreciatively. 'Ready to go?' he asked.

All at once Danni remembered his mode of transport and hesitated. Surely he must have come by car? He didn't look at all windswept himself.

His eyebrows were raised. 'What's the hold-up?'

'I was going to change,' Danni began.

'Change?' He looked at her dress and she blushed again under his gaze. 'No need to change. You look fine. Very sexy,' he grinned.

'But . . . I forgot about your motorcycle,' she told him. 'I'm not dressed to ride pillion.'

His grin widened. 'We're going in style tonight, Miss Mathieson. I have a car, believe it or not. Okay?'

Danni smiled with relief and picking up her evening bag followed him out of the door, locking it behind her.

In the glow of the street light a low green sedan glistened in the semi-darkness. The shape was unfamiliar, but it had the look of speed.

'Could you really see me riding a motorcycle in this outfit?' Shiloh asked as he held open her door.

Pausing as she stepped into the car, Danni looked

at him and had a mental picture of him riding through town and the surprised looks he would have been given, and laughed. 'I'll bet you'd have collected a few comments!' She sank into the bucket seat, impressed by the car's immaculate condition.

Shiloh closed the door and walked around to the driver's side. In the glow of the interior light the badge of the steering wheel caught Danni's eye. Lotus. No wonder the car had looked racy! The engine came to life with the quiet control of a thorough-bred and when Shiloh turned on the lights Danni watched in fascination as the headlights rose from their position flush with the bonnet. She glanced sideways at Shiloh and he pushed another switch. Her window slid smoothly down and then up again.

He shrugged his shoulders and chuckled. 'Man must have his toys,' he said.

'How long have you had the Lotus? An Elan, isn't it?' Danni asked, trying to drag her eyes from his hands skilfully and easily manipulating the steering wheel.

'Yes, an Elan plus two. I've had it a couple of years now,' he replied. 'It was somewhat ill-used when I bought it and I was almost through restoring it when I—er—when I had to leave it for a while. It was all ready for its final coat of paint, so a friend of mine, who was helping me with it at the time, went ahead with it and it was ready for me when I got back. We finished off the mechanical bits and pieces a few weeks ago.'

There was a few moments' silence.

'Have you always been interested in driving fast cars?' Danni asked him.

'Not always. I really wanted to be a fireman.' He was smiling. 'That was before I went to a go-kart meeting with a couple of mates. I was just a bit of a kid and I started out driving the go-karts. They were a lot of fun and from there I went into fast bikes, with which I was quite satisfied until I discovered fast women.'

Danni could see the creases in his cheek deepen as she watched his profile in the subdued light of the instrument panel.

'It soon became obvious to me,' he continued, 'that the fast women didn't care to be taken about on the back of a fast bike, so the natural progression was to fast cars. How about you? Always hankered after speed?'

Danni laughed. 'Well, my first recollections are of steering a battered old station utility across a paddock while perched on Pop's knee. That was before we came down from the north to Mallaroo, so I must have been about five or six. I'm afraid I can't claim any fast men,' she chuckled. 'It was nothing more exciting than one fast brother taking me with him in his saloon car on a practice run around the Surfers track. I was about fourteen and I must admit that I was exhilaratedly terrified.

'We kind of failed to mention the outing to Pop and when I'd been going with Rick for about three weeks someone let the cat out of the bag—and wow, did Pop hit the roof! He really hauled Rick over the coals and made me promise never to go again unless he came with us.'

'And do the fast cars still terrify you?'

'Not exactly terrify.' Danni frowned, trying to analyse her feelings on the subject. 'I know that I can handle the car, Rick saw to that. And I know I can trust the car mechanically as I have a mechanic who's one of the best. How I'll fare in the competition remains to be seen, but I'm confident.'

They were lost in their own thoughts as Shiloh pulled up smoothly at a red light.

'How long did you know Rick?' Danni asked when they had rejoined the traffic flow.

There was a tense pause before he answered. 'The first time we met must have been all of—oh, fourteen years ago. I was racing motorcycles then. Just before the fast women entered the scene,' his laugh was a trifle forced. 'Rick was a few years older than I was and driving his own saloon car, an old Holden, I think. We ran into each other on and off for a few years at the tracks until I left the scene for a while when I was twenty.'

He pulled easily around a car that had halted in his path. 'I went to the U.K. for a while.' He paused again, as though he felt he was treading on uneven ground. 'A working holiday.'

'Were you there long?' Danni probed, sensing the tenseness in the man beside her and not understanding the reason for it.

'About eight years. I returned to Aussie after four years, but I hadn't been back long when I was offered a job back over there. I had hoped to begin racing here, but I accepted the position in the U.K., mainly because of the opportunity to gain invaluable experience in engineering.' He pulled into a small parking area behind a narrow building just outside the main shopping centre of Surfers Paradise.

The restaurant, the Old Coach House, was in the basement of a tall building of business offices. Danni had not been there before and Shiloh took her arm as they walked downstairs, telling her that his friend had only taken over the business two months previously. He had redecorated the place inside and was now building up his clientele.

Inside, the restaurant was larger than the impression given by the stairway leading down to it. The muted-toned walls were decorated with old sepia prints of approximately poster size. The tables were set in intimate alcoves as well as in the main section of the room and a band played subdued background music. The antique design of the hanging lights in amber and black gave a very pleasing atmosphere of old-world charm.

A waiter led them to a table in the seclusion of an alcove and Danni gazed with interest at the old print over their table which bore the label 'Surfers Paradise 1930'. To Danni the scene was unrecognisable. They sipped a light wine after the waiter had departed with their order and they were discussing the old print and the rate of change in the Gold Coast area when a short grey-haired man of Danni's father's vintage approached their table. The newcomer smiled at Danni and shook Shiloh's hand enthusiastically.

'Welcome back, Rourkey. Good to see you on your feet again.' The man sat down on a chair he took from a vacant table behind him.

A little tinkling bell of memory rang in the back of Danni's mind and slipped away again as she reached out to grasp it.

'Good to see you, too, Bill,' Shiloh turned to Danni. 'This is an old friend, Bill Peterson, who owns this set-up. Bill, meet Danni Mathieson.'

'Glad to meet you, Miss Mathieson.' Bill Peterson stood up to shake her hand and then subsided into the chair. 'I know you'll enjoy your meal. I've got the best chef in the area.' He smiled and turned back to Shiloh. 'How did you go in Brisbane? Success?'

Out of the corner of her eye Danni saw Shiloh make an almost imperceptible shake of his head while he casually replied to the question. 'As I told you when I rang, I was only expecting moderate success. That's about what I got.'

Bill Peterson nodded in agreement, a faintly puzzled look in his eyes as he glanced quickly at Danni and back to Shiloh.

'How about a glass of wine, Bill? Danni and I are celebrating.' Shiloh filled a glass for the other man, who along with Danni, was gazing questioningly at him. Shiloh lifted his glass and said teasingly, 'This is our first night out together. And what's more, I had to persuade Danni to come, much against her better judgment, didn't I, Danni?'

Before Danni could comment Bill Peterson laughed. 'And I can understand her reticence, too, even if you have had a haircut since I saw you last. I guess you must be responsible for that, Miss Mathieson. Although I must admit he does look resplendent in that get-up.'

'I may have lost my strength with my hair,' Shiloh pulled a face, and turned to Danni. 'What do you say, Delilah?'

Flipping her own hair back from her face, Danni set her mouth primly. 'You're rather old to be trying to carry off the "angry young man" bit.' She watched to see whether her barbs went home.

He threw back his head and laughed. 'Ah, Danni,' he placed one hand on his heart, 'you sure know how to hurt a fellow. Here I am, an old man at thirty. What's left for me in life but an armchair by the fire?'

'Maybe you should settle for that,' laughed Bill. 'Especially if someone like Miss Mathieson was around to fetch you your slippers.'

'There's food for thought.' Shiloh's cat's eyes twinkled.

'Please call me Danni,' she smiled at Bill Peterson to cover her embarrassment. '"Miss Mathieson" makes *me* feel old.'

'Thanks, Danni.' He inclined his head. 'Mathieson?' he hesitated, his eyes moving quickly back to Shiloh.

'Danni's Jock Mathieson's daughter,' Shiloh told him quickly.

Something passed between the two men before Bill turned to Danni. 'Well now, how is old Jock? I've met him at the race track every so often over the years. Owns a farm up this way, doesn't he?'

'Yes. Mallaroo Downs is up in the Valley, but he often comes down to the coast. We have a house at Broadbeach. I'll tell him you asked after him.'

'I'd appreciate that, Danni. Perhaps you could ask him to give me a call when he's next in town? As you grow older you enjoy renewing old acquaintances,' he smiled reminiscently.

At that moment a young waiter appeared with a message for Bill and he excused himself reluctantly, telling them to be sure to enjoy their evening.

And to Danni's surprise the evening flew by. She had half expected that an evening spent in Shiloh's company would be one of conflict and irritation, but in this assumption she was totally mistaken. They found much in common to discuss and the fine food, the atmosphere of the restaurant, coupled with fine wine mellowed them both.

Danni had visited various places in England with which Shiloh was familiar and they swapped experiences and reminiscences with companionable enjoy-

ment. Their tastes in music and literature were similar enough and Shiloh seemed to have the knack of
drawing Danni out, although it wasn't until later
that she realised he deftly managed to change the
subject whenever it veered near motor racing. Part-
way through the evening she realised she was
actually coming to like this more serious Shiloh
O'Rourke and, in fact, he hadn't provoked her all
evening.

They had finished dessert and sat back replete
when the band which had been playing during the
evening began another bracket of dance music, and
they made their way to the microscopic dance floor
where they joined a number of other couples in a
medium to fast bout of disco music.

They had gyrated themselves through two songs
when Danni remembered noticing Shiloh's limp as
they were crossing the road to the library that afternoon. He hadn't mentioned it and suddenly she was
loath to, some sixth sense telling her that touching
on the subject might in some way change the timbre
of what was an enjoyable evening. Surely he would
say something if his leg was troubling him. She
watched him closely for a few minutes and, although
he was favouring his stronger leg, he didn't seem to
be suffering any ill effects from the strenuous dance.

He caught her eyes on him and she felt herself
blushing under that same devastating smile. Reluctantly she admitted to herself that it wasn't the energy
she was expending on the intricate dance steps that
was wholly responsible for her sudden breath-
lessness.

The band's tempo changed to a slow romantic
ballad and Shiloh pulled her closer into a more con-
ventional hold.

'This is one of my favourite songs,' she told the front of his ruffled shirt, the touch of his hands warm on her back, burning through the thin material of her dress.

'Mmm,' Shiloh murmured softly into her dark hair, its clean healthy silkiness feeling pleasant against his cheek.

'It's one of Dr Hook's,' she told him, her throat suddenly dry as the tension between them mounted.

'Mmm,' he said again.

'I don't suppose you've heard of Dr Hook,' she persevered. 'It's a group.'

'As it so happens,' he said huskily, drawing her still closer, 'I have heard of Dr Hook, so maybe I'm younger than you'd think by looking at my ancient face.' He drew back a little and smiled down into her eyes.

She smiled back, relaxing instinctively into the circle of his arms.

'That's better,' he whispered appreciatively, and they leaned against each other, scarcely moving at all.

The touch of Shiloh's body so close to her own was having a breathtaking effect on Danni. It seemed as though she could feel every muscular contour of his body. She had never danced this closely with a man before. Oh, she had danced cheek to cheek, but never in this totally sensual, intimate contiguity.

Her hands were resting on his chest, her fingers twined in the softness of his shirt, and the clean masculine scent of spicy aftershave lotion was almost intoxicating. The firmness of his thighs, flexing in slow movements to the rhythm of the music, had her heart racing while his arms wrapped about her body held her locked to him. Danni gave herself up to the stimulating newness of their mutual arousal, and when the bracket of romantic music ended they remained close together for some seconds before they realised that the other couples were leaving the floor.

Shiloh stepped back and sighed. 'Pity Dr Hook's songs weren't hours longer,' he murmured, his eyes alight with an expression that had Danni's senses soaring and, taking her hand, he led her back to their table.

CHAPTER THREE

DANNI felt she was walking along on cloud nine. Her whole body seemed to be tuned to the tall man walking beside her, his hand clasping hers, his shoulder touching hers. Tonight she was seeing a totally different side to this unconventional man, a side that had probably been in evidence when she had first made his acquaintance had she but allowed herself to see it. What was more, she knew in her heart that he could very easily become important to her, and this feeling was causing her some apprehension. She shivered as she sat down opposite him. Somehow she wasn't ready to want to make or need any commitments. Everything was moving too fast for her. Her heart flipped over while her head bade her hesitate.

Until this evening her whole life, all her energies, revolved around her motor racing. She gave no time or thought to anything else save her job. Romance just didn't enter into her scheme of things, not until she had taken out the series and had tried her luck and skill overseas.

They chatted on as before, and yet not quite as before. A spark had been added to their relationship and it glowed brightly in both their eyes. They each knew it was there and for their own reasons tried to keep it in its place. For Danni the feeling was too new to her and her natural reticence kept a tight rein on her so that she was almost relieved when the time eventually came for them to leave.

Excusing herself, Danni went to the powder room to touch up her make-up and tidy her hair. She gazed into the mirror, her eyes almost the shade of violets as they glowed with a new awareness. No other man had ever made her feel this way. It was as though all her senses were stimulated to fever pitch. And if her eyes glowed mistily then a flush of rose touched her cheeks while her lips trembled with a hitherto unknown yearning.

Would he kiss her goodnight? Her knees turned to water at the thought and she clutched at the bench top for support. Good grief, she was behaving like a teenager on her first date! A tiny flame of pleasure rose from deep inside her and she knew that she wanted him to kiss her, to take possession of her lips with his own, and that feeling had nothing of a teenager in it, it was all woman.

Danni splashed her burning cheeks with cool water and dried her face on a paper towel. Where was the single-minded, controlled motor racer now? She renewed her lipstick and, taking her emotions firmly in hand, opened the door and looked about in search of that now super-familiar figure.

He had told her he would chat to Bill while he waited for her and it only took her a few seconds to place him across the room. She wended her way across to them and as she approached she noticed the two men deep in conversation. Their faces were serious and Bill was shaking his head in a kind of sympathetic disbelief. When Shiloh caught sight of her he changed the topic of their conversation, his face once more full of humour, an emotion that had been missing from his expression a few moments earlier.

They said their farewells and set off across the restaurant to the door to the street, and Danni became

aware that more than one pair of feminine eyes
followed Shiloh's figure as they moved through the
tables.

Everything seemed to have taken on a rosy mag-
nification in the few hours they had spent together.
Her eyes were continually drawn to him, her
thoughts were centred around him, were full of him,
and her heart had developed a disturbing miss-beat
whenever their eyes met or they touched. Danni
grinned happily to herself.

'What was that secret little smile for back in the
restaurant, Miss Mathieson?' Shiloh asked teasingly
as he fastened his seatbelt.

Danni blushed in the covering darkness. 'I was
only thinking about the wonderful meal,' she improvised guiltily.

'I'm glad you enjoyed it,' he said easily as the
engine throbbed to life.

They spoke occasionally on the short journey back
to Broadbeach and in no time they were turning
into Danni's street. Shiloh pulled the car into the
kerb in front of the house and switched off the ignition. The car's interior was dimly lit by the panel
lights and Danni's heartbeat had accelerated as she
fumbled nervously with the buckle of her seatbelt.

Shiloh flipped off his own harness and reached
across to help her with hers. His hands moved over
hers and the buckle was undone. Her hand was still
clasped in his and with a sigh he leaned back in his
own seat, keeping hold of her hand. Her fingers
naturally twined with his and she turned her head
so that she could watch him in the semi-darkness.

Danni's body was stiff with tension, her overriding
emotion one of disinclination to have the evening
end. Shiloh turned to look at her and she knew he

was smiling. Some of her tension seemed to leave her, although her heartbeats still continued to race.

'Thanks for a great evening, Danni,' he said quietly. 'I haven't enjoyed myself so much in ages. Glad I talked you into coming?' he asked.

'Yes, I'm glad I came. I've enjoyed it, too.' Danni's voice sounded unnatural to her ears.

He raised her hand to his lips, kissing her softly on her palm. At the burning touch of those lips her fingers curled strongly within his. Her eyes flew to his face and in the confines of the car the flame of attraction between them sparked and ignited.

She heard him murmur her name huskily before his lips found hers in the darkness. As they touched passion flared between them. The forcefulness of possession in that kiss took Danni momentarily by surprise, but her senses responded involuntarily to his demands. It was a response she had never given before to any man and the wonder of her feelings filled her with a fear that had about it a touch of bittersweetness. It was all happening far too quickly. Her hands were crushed between their bodies and as the sensation of fear reached her consciousness she pushed her hands against him while her lips parted beneath his in spontaneous surrender.

Reluctantly Shiloh lifted his lips from hers. His fingers were twined in her hair and he brought her head closer to him so that his lips rested against her temple.

Trembling in his arms, Danni yearned to feel the touch of his lips on hers once more, but somehow she was afraid of the path along which this might lead. She felt very young and naïve, but recognised from the slight trembling of his own body that he was keeping himself under tight control.

His lips moved slowly down to her earlobe, over-whelming her senses to such an extent that she was unable to control the surge of response which swelled and engulfed her. All thought of resistance dis-appeared and she turned her face until her lips could feel the ecstasy of his touch once again. His kiss probed and gently teased as their ardour rose.

In the darkness of Danni's mind a little bell tinkled warningly, but she was too carried away on the wave of her response to pay heed. The strap of her dress was pushed from her shoulder and his lips left a trail of fire over the smoothness of her skin to the hollow at her throat where a pulse throbbed her heightened awareness of this man's attraction. His lips moved downwards to the valley between her breasts while his hands caressed her, burning through the material of her dress. That material was all at once an en-cumbrance. He wanted to touch her without the thickness of the material between them, and she wanted it too.

He moved to get closer to her, only to knock his knee sharply on the console between the seats. Biting off an epithet, he raised himself so that his body, the upper part at least, was against hers.

Danni strained nearer, her hands slipping inside the softness of his shirt, moving sensuously over his firm skin, now slightly damp with their lovemaking. His own hands moved over her creating havoc with her senses.

How long their next kiss lasted Danni couldn't have told. Perhaps it would have gone on for ever. But a car coming towards them flashed its headlights on to high beam and the brightness of those lights in Danni's eyes brought her down to earth as the warning bells began to ring again with increased intensity. When Shiloh went to draw her back into his arms she held back, resting her forehead against his lips while she pulled the strap of her dress back into place.

He sensed the change in her and placing a hand on either side of her face looked into her eyes, large and bright; at her lips, swollen and trembling from his kisses. For a moment Danni thought he would pull her into his arms again, but instead he smiled down at her a little ruefully and kissed her gently on the tip of her nose.

'I know you're right, sweetie, but at this moment I sure wish you weren't,' he said huskily, and moved over into his own seat, keeping her hand clasped in his. He laughed softly. 'Believe it or not, I fully intended to shake your hand and bid you a chaste goodnight. Well, perhaps I thought a nice friendly kiss on the cheek might have been in order.' His voice smiled. 'My intentions let me down miserably, didn't they?' His fingers gently played with hers. 'Must have been the devil on my shoulder whispering wicked thoughts into my ear.'

A smile tugged at Danni's mouth. 'He must have been whispering in mine as well,' she said shakily.

He reached out and gently touched her lips with one finger and she pursed her lips against it in a soft kiss.

Shiloh's eyes blazed, reminding her once again of a jungle cat's. 'Danni,' he said in a tortured voice, 'don't look at me like that or I won't have the strength to leave you tonight.' He closed his eyes and rested his head back against the headrest.

The way Danni felt at the moment she could have curled up in the contoured comfort of the Lotus beside this man until the end of time. Had anyone suggested last weekend that she would be sitting with this particular man, the imprint of his lips still filling her with newly awakened yearnings, she would have been the first to scoff at the incongruity of it. In fact, if anyone had told her how it would be even half an hour before Shiloh had called for her this evening she would have laughed in disbelief. Perhaps the feelings of what she had thought was dislike had all the while been sparks of physical attraction.

She looked at the firm lines of Shiloh's profile and a tide of feeling rose within her so that she had to prevent herself from reaching across to touch the chiselled strength of his features. It's too soon, cried an inner voice, and Danni moved slightly in a fever of indecision, admitting to herself that she desperately wanted to know more of this man.

Her movement brought Shiloh's eyes back to her face. 'I guess I should let you go inside. You have to go to work tomorrow and I can imagine your friend—what was her name? Lisa? I can imagine what kind of connotation she would put on our evening if you turned up late with your eyelids propped open.'

Danni laughed. He was right about that. 'I'm on late shift tomorrow,' she told him. 'I don't start until ten-thirty and I finish at eight o'clock.'

'Well, I could keep you here for ages yet, with a clear conscience,' he squeezed her hand, 'except for the fact that I have to be in Brisbane tomorrow at nine o'clock, with all my faculties about me.'

Danni sat forward in concern, glancing at the luminous dial of her wristwatch. 'It's almost one o'clock,' she said in surprise. 'I didn't realise it was so late. It feels as though it should be eleven at the very latest.'

'Time has flown, Danni my love, while we've been

having fun.' He shifted stiffly in his seat, rubbing his leg as though he had suffered a cramp. 'Come on, I'll walk you safely to your door.'

They walked up the path, his hand resting lightly on her waist and the soft silkiness of his shirt brushing her arm. He took her key from her and unlocked the door, reaching inside to switch on the light in the foyer of the old Colonial-style home. Taking her chin in one hand, he moved his lips gently on hers for one heart-stopping moment.

'Mmm. Danni, you're bewitching. I wish ...' he paused. 'I wish I didn't have to go away tomorrow.' He sighed. 'Something tells me I should spirit you away to a deserted atoll somewhere on the Great Barrier Reef. We could sit back and let the whole crazy world sail by without us.'

Danni smiled, her hand clasped in his. 'That's always been a dream of mine, to live on a tropic isle somewhere far away from the rat race. Blue skies, white sands, green coconut palms, Robert Redford,' she laughed. 'I think I read *The Swiss Family Robinson* at a very impressionable age.'

'Me, too,' Shiloh laughed with her. 'We'll have to explore the idea further when I get back.' He looked down at her. 'Robert Redford indeed! We have an old saying peculiar to the O'Rourke clan which goes, and I quote, "One Shiloh O'Rourke in the hand is worth two Robert Redfords on the screen".'

Danni laughed and leaned against him. 'How long do you expect to be in the city?' she asked, happy in the thrill of knowing he wanted to see her again.

In the shaft of light falling through the open door-way from the foyer his expression barely changed, only the smile in his eyes faded. Had she not been looking again at their unusual colour she would have missed that subtle variation. As it was, the change was so fleeting that she thought she might have imagined it.

'I'm not exactly sure,' he replied carefully. 'I'm flying down to Sydney from Brisbane and, at the moment, I hope to be back some time next week. Maybe Wednesday.'

'Oh.' Danni's heart sank. All of a sudden the thought of not seeing him for a week was dejecting.

He pulled her closer, locking his arms about her and resting his chin lightly on top of her head. 'Don't tell me you'll miss me?' he asked softly, lifting his head so that he could look into her eyes.

Her eyes moved over his face, drinking in each feature, committing every part of it to memory, afraid of the tumult of feelings that threatened to engulf her. A feeling akin to panic rose within her and once again she shied away from making a commitment, from putting into words what she suspected was going to be the understatement of the year. Somehow she had a foreboding that she would find the days while he was away unusually long and lifeless.

His proprietorial smile told her he had read her mind and he lowered his lips to hers in a lingering kiss. The kiss began as a gentle and tender goodbye, but somehow deepened until they clung convulsively together, carried away on a tide of desire that neither of them tried to control or wanted to abate. Danni could feel the tension in his thighs burning through the thin material of her dress and her own legs turned to water. Then he had put a space between them, his breathing ragged, as though he had been running a long distance. Danni felt their separation as a physical wrench.

Shiloh shook his head in what was almost disbelief. 'I think I should be gone, Danni, otherwise we'll be here all night, and I mean that quite literally.'

Her face flamed at the meaning behind his words and she knew with a shock that she would not resist him if he did want to stay. He touched his finger to his lips, then placed his finger against Danni's lips. 'I wish I could make it back for your race at the weekend. What time will you get home on Sunday night?' he asked softly.

'Not late. I should be home by seven. We take the car back out to Mallaroo, then I stay the night and come back for work on Monday morning,' she told him.

'Fine. I'll ring you there at about eight o'clock if I can get to a phone.' He went down the steps and strode up the path. At the gate he turned and raised one hand and before Danni could move the red glow of his tail lights was disappearing down the street.

With a bemused half smile on her face she walked inside and locked the door after her, her arms wrapping themselves about her body in sheer wonderful pleasure.

You don't know a thing about him, said a voice inside her, but she refused to listen. She was riding too high on the heavenly cloud on to which Shiloh had lifted her with his kisses. Her smile widened and she didn't give her previous misgivings another thought.

Danni scarcely had time to stow her bag in her locker in the staffroom next morning before Lisa came rushing in all agog. Danni was expecting Lisa's inquisition and had prepared herself to answer innumerable questions.

'At last you're here, Danni. I've been beside

myself with curiosity all morning to find out how your evening went,' began the other girl. 'Where did you go? What did you wear? What was he like?'

'Lisa, please!' Danni held up her hand. 'How can I answer your questions when you race them in one after another?'

'Sorry, Danni, but you know how excited I've been for you.'

'I don't know why, Lisa. I've only known the man for a week.' Danni kept her voice matter-of-fact. When she actually put that fact into words it seemed unbelievable. In truth, she had only known Shiloh for a week, less than a week, while she felt as though they had known each other for ever.

'That's by the way,' Lisa was saying offhandedly. 'All it takes is a moment and, as I said before, I have a feeling about this.' Her eyes held a dreamy look of impending romance.

Danni shook her head in mock exasperation as the head librarian walked into the room.

'Morning, Danni. I hope you'll give Lisa all the details. We haven't had a coherent word out of her all morning,' remarked Sue, who was thirty-six and happily married with two teenage children.

'Well, there isn't much to tell. We went to the Old Coach House restaurant in Surfers Paradise, we dined, talked and danced and then he took me home.'

Sue smiled as Lisa's face fell.

'But, Danni, was that all?' Lisa's voice was filled with disappointment.

'You've read too many romances and watched too many movies.' Danni winked across at Sue, feeling a bit of a fraud. 'What else did you expect? That we'd elope and live happily ever after?'

'Elope? Danni, you wouldn't elope, would you?' Lisa's face showed horror. 'You wouldn't do us out of a perfectly good wedding when you know how we love them?'

Sue and Danni burst out laughing.

'Lisa, you make me feel like reaching for my walking stick and crocheted shawl,' remarked Sue as she returned to the library proper to attend to a borrower.

'Come on, Danni,' begged Lisa. 'Please tell me about your evening.'

Sighing, Danni picked up a list of books she had to check. 'I did have a very good evening, Lisa. I wore my blue crêpe dress, the one I bought about two weeks ago when we went up to Pacific Fair, and we had a delicious meal. There was a very nice band playing and a small dance floor, so we danced and talked some more. In fact, we found we had quite a lot in common.'

'Oh, Danni, I'm so glad! He's so handsome,' Lisa beamed.

'Don't let your imagination run away with you now. We went out once and had a very enjoyable time, that's all.' Danni stated emphatically, as much for her own benefit as Lisa's.

'What happened when he took you home? Did he kiss you goodnight?'

To her annoyance Danni felt herself blushing. 'Lisa! You are the nosiest person I know. What a thing to ask!'

'Well, did he?' The other girl was unrepentant.

'Well, what do you think?' Danni tried to brazen it out.

'Judging by your blush I'd say he did kiss you goodnight, and very satisfactorily, too,' Lisa chuckled. 'Don't worry, Danni, your secret is safe with me,' she teased.

Danni tried to look reprimanding but ended up laughing reluctantly. 'You really are incorrigible!'

'When are you seeing him again?' Lisa asked, unabashed.

'Next week, maybe,' Danni replied cautiously.

'Next week?' Lisa raised her eyebrows. 'And why maybe? I thought you said you enjoyed yourself?'

'I did enjoy myself, and "next week" because he's going, has gone, down to Sydney on business and won't be back until Wednesday at least,' explained Danni. She made no mention of Shiloh's prospective telephone call on Sunday in case it didn't eventuate. She mustn't build that phone call up into anything more than it was.

'What sort of business is he in?' asked Lisa.

Danni did a double take. 'Actually, I'm not sure. I can't remember him mentioning anything about his business. Oh, it must be in engineering. He did say he spent some time in the U.K. in some position to do with engineering.'

'Mmm.' Lisa frowned. 'Well, it's bad timing on his part, this business trip. How does he know you won't get snapped up in the meantime?'

'Snapped up?' Danni laughed gaily. 'By whom, pray?'

'You never know, do you? Anyone could walk into the library, take one look at you, and that would be that. For that matter, what about the ever faithful Dallas Byrne? If you raised your little finger he'd come running, you know that,' reminded Lisa.

'And you know that I'm not interested in Dallas in that way,' replied Danni. 'I like Dallas very much, but as a friend, nothing more. It could never be any more than that.' Especially after last night, a little voice whispered secretly in her heart.

Lisa nodded. 'Poor Dallas! He'll just have to learn to live with that, although I can tell he hasn't given up on you yet. You know, Dallas's whole trouble is that he's too nice. He's not bad looking, allowing for his red hair, so I'm sure if he tried a bit of the cave-man stuff you'd think more of him. He sits back and lets you make all the running when he would have been better off telling you that you were going with him and that was that.'

'I can't, by any stretch of the imagination, im-agine Dallas hitting a girl over the head with a club and dragging her off by the hair. He's much too gentle.' Danni was amused. 'And I'm not sure that I care for tough stuff much. There has to be a happy medium to be found somewhere. Anyway, how come all of a sudden you're regaling me with Dallas's virtues when a moment ago you had me all but married to Shiloh O'Rourke?'

Lisa's brow puckered in thought. 'Now that I come to think of it,' she said seriously, 'it has to be Shiloh O'Rourke for you. I've read all the signs and they're written there on your face. You've never blushed over Dallas, neither have you become de-cidedly vague when discussing him or anyone else. Usually, you're sharp as a tack about even the most minute detail. With Shiloh O'Rourke you're all fluffy-headed and distant. Yes, it has to be Shiloh O'Rourke.' She gave Danni a studiedly direct look and then went off to answer the telephone.

The phone call was for Danni, so she didn't have long to meditate upon Lisa's statements. Her heart began to thump painfully. Maybe Shiloh ...? No, it couldn't possibly be him. He would be in mid-air between Brisbane and Sydney by now. She took the phone from Lisa, who completely burst the bubble by mouthing that it was Dallas.

'Danni?' asked his familiar voice. 'Hi! It's me, Dallas. Sorry to disturb you at work. I rang you at home last night but couldn't get you. What's the arrangement for tomorrow?'

Danni blinked. Tomorrow? Oh, the races. How could she have forgotten? Until the last day or so the first motor races of the new series had been the focal point in her life. She had been practising and working towards these races for months.

'Oh, the races, of course,' she said absently.

'Danni, that is you, isn't it?' On the other end of the line Dallas's voice was filled with puzzlement.

'Yes, Dallas, it is me. Who else?' She forced a laugh into her voice. 'Now, I'm working in the morning until twelve, so I guess you'll have to bring the car down and I'll meet you at the track at about twelve-thirty.'

'Okay, will do. I hope you aren't nervous about the races, Danni, are you?' His voice held concern. 'You don't sound like you today.'

'No, of course not, Dallas. I won't be nervous until I'm on the starting grid. I'm sorry I was so vague. I had my mind lost in a list of books I was reading off.' Danni grimaced as Lisa raised her eyebrows at Danni's slight bending of the truth.

'Well, I'm nervous enough for both of us,' Dallas was saying, 'but I suppose you'll be as cool as a cucumber. You usually are. I don't know how you manage it.'

'If you keep telling me I won't be nervous, Dallas, I'll do an about-face and go completely to pieces!'

'Hey, Danni, don't do that,' Dallas said quickly, all concern.

'I was only teasing, Dallas,' she took pity on him, wishing he would relax and let himself enjoy a joke occasionally. It wasn't that he was stuffy or boring, but he never seemed to be able to laugh at himself. 'I promise not to be nervous. Are you sure you don't mind bringing the car down from Mallaroo without my help? I would have changed my shift with Sue, but she has her sister's wedding tomorrow.'

'No, it's all right, Danni,' Dallas hastened to reassure her. 'I'm free in the morning, so I'll take my time. One of the boys will give me a hand. Does your father know not to expect you home this evening?'

'Yes. I phoned him as soon as I knew I'd be working in the morning,' Danni told him. 'Pop will help you get everything ready.'

'Good. I can have everything set up by the time you get out to the track. The first practice heats for the Formula Fords are at two o'clock, aren't they? You're number fifty-two, so I guess you'll be in the second heat. There won't be any need for you to hurry down.'

'Thanks, Dallas, that'll be fine. See you tomorrow, then.' And he rang off.

Danni replaced the receiver on its cradle.

'Poor Dallas,' Lisa shook her head. 'He doesn't stand a chance, does he?'

A picture of Shiloh O'Rourke appeared vividly in Danni's mind as she looked at the younger girl, and she sighed. 'No, Lisa, I guess he doesn't, at that.'

CHAPTER FOUR

THE following afternoon Danni sat comfortably on a collapsible aluminium chair, reading her novel. She found reading the most relaxing way to spend the time waiting for her practice heats to be run. There was much activity all about, and the activity was all automobile-orientated. The throb of engines hung heavy on the clear air in the paddock.

It was an ideal day for racing. The sky was blue, broken here and there by light fluffy white clouds, and the weather report predicted another fine day for tomorrow's racing. A cool fresh breeze stirred the flowing green grass in the wide expanse enclosed by the track. The breeze lifted Danni's hair as she sat in the shade of the tarpaulin awning they had erected out from the utility. She wore her driving suit, which was a bright shade of lime green, the reflected colours giving her eyes the turquoise shade of the sea less than ten kilometres from the raceway.

There was nearly an hour for Danni to wait for her heats on the track and Dallas professed the car to be ready to go. The car had been passed as safe and legally complying with the race rules by the officials, and at the moment Dallas was giving it a final check-over. Danni smiled tolerantly at him as he fussed about the car like a mother hen. From the pocket of his light blue overalls he pulled a soft cloth and began to buff up the already gleaming paintwork. She shook her head, knowing his actions to be a release of nervous tension and pre-race jitters, which she surprisingly hadn't yet begun to suffer. On the starting grid she admitted to a certain fluttering of butterflies in her stomach, but once on the track her thoughts and reactions were highly tuned to the race and her handling of her car.

She ran her eye over the Lola. The majority of the bodywork was painted a bright lemon yellow, which contrasted acutely with the black of the tyres. Both sides and the bonnet of the car bore a large white circle with the number fifty-two, which was Danni's allotted number, clearly displayed. Advertisements for her sponsors were marked on the sides towards the rear and across the bonnet, Mallaroo Stud and a brand of motor oil which gave generous encouragement to a large number of amateur drivers.

Danni shifted slightly in her chair, her eyes returning to her novel. She was all ready to climb into the car, except for her headgear and gloves. Her father had made her a gift of her racing outfit, although she had a sneaking suspicion that he was not totally happy about her racing. However, he had sponsored her car, and taken Dallas on as a part-time hand at Mallaroo and part-time mechanic for the T.A.A. Formula Ford Driver to Europe series in which Danni was entered.

The fact that the rounds of the series were run in each state meant a considerable amount of travelling for Dallas and Danni. She had not wanted to throw in her job at the library, so she had worked out a rather tight schedule for herself. Dallas would drive the utility and the trailered racer down to each racetrack and set everything up while Danni flew down on Friday night when she finished work. She would return by plane on Sunday night, ready for work on Monday. Fortunately, there were only four rounds in the series, stretched out over three months. During the rest of the season she would compete in the State titles run at Surfers Paradise International Raceway and at Lakeside.

Danni glanced at her wristwatch and then across to see Dallas, his polishing cloth back in his pocket, heading her way.

'Time to get ready.' Dallas joined her, handing her her balaclava and helmet. 'You feel okay, Danni?' he asked, full of his usual concern. 'Not too nervous, are you?'

'No, Dallas, I'm fine,' she replied, slipping her safety helmet on to her head and adjusting the chin-straps. 'Keep your fingers crossed for me!'

She slid into the body-moulding contours of the cockpit and Dallas helped her fasten and adjust her racing harness. A voice on the loudspeaker crackled out almost incoherently and Dallas nodded his head, giving her the thumbs up. The engine roared to life and Danni returned his signal, grinning behind her helmet. Dallas's face cracked into what he occa-sionally used as his encouraging smile, he gave the car a push to start her on her way and she idled the car out through the gateway and on to the track.

Surprisingly she didn't feel at all nervous. This was the day she had been waiting for, and somehow it was a bit of an anticlimax. She had discussed her idea of being the first female Formula Ford driver to win the 'Driver to Europe' series, which was sponsored by a major airline, with her brother, and he had been enthusiastically all for it. It seemed such a long time ago now and suddenly she felt very alone. She turned her head towards the pits and there was

Dallas's red head shining in the sunlight. He gave her a quick salute and she felt immediately calmer. The roar of the other Formula Ford engines was almost deafening and the stewards waved the cars on to the track for their warm-up lap. Danni took the car at a steady pace around the circuit, under Dunlop Bridge and along Peters straight and back to the starting grid.

It was just after dark on Sunday evening when they finally locked the Lola in the shed and climbed wearily into the utility for the short drive up to the house.

'Pity I couldn't have made it a first instead of a second,' mused Danni.

'Your second was fantastic enough.' Dallas's voice was full of pride. 'I knew Casey Jones was the only one you had to get in front of, and our tactics to get under him on Datsun corner really paid off. Ninety-nine per cent of the time he swung out wide there and if you hadn't had to swerve around that spin out on Goodyear Casey wouldn't have got that fraction in front. Another lap and you'd have had him. Anyway, second's not to be laughed at at this stage. It's a healthy start to the series. We'll get him next time. I reckon you're going to be the first woman to take it out.'

'We'll see, Dallas. I wish I was as confident as you are.' And I wish it meant as much to me as it did a week ago, if only for your sake, she added to herself.

'What made you invite that kid back today, Danni?' Dallas grumbled. 'Most of the afternoon Saturday and then today. Who was he anyway?'

'Nathan? He came looking for me because his brother knew me. I—er—I met him the other day,' Danni replied vaguely. She had been quite taken aback when Shiloh's young brother came up to her.

'Yes, well, I expected we'd have the time together, talk about the race, plan our strategy in peace. And instead we had to put up with his incessant chatter.'

'Dallas, don't be so grumpy,' Danni half laughed. 'Nathan's a nice boy. Besides, you should be flattered. He thinks you know it all about cars. Second only to his brother, of course.'

'Yes, this brother of his, this Shiloh, what's he like? I mean, how old is he? And how do you come to know him?' Dallas had turned slightly sideways on in the passenger seat and was looking at her watchfully.

'He seems quite nice. He's around about thirty. And I don't know him all that well,' Danni finished tersely, feeling suddenly inexplicably guilty under Dallas's unsmiling gaze.

'Shiloh?' Dallas repeated sarcastically. 'I guess it must be his real name. No one could make that up.'

'Dallas—!' Danni began.

'Well, how did you come to meet him?' Dallas turned back to her.

She sighed. 'He was riding past Mallaroo last weekend when I was practising and he stopped to— er—look at the car,' she improvised.

'You mean he just walked in off the street? A stranger?' said Dallas incredulously. 'And you didn't send him on his way? Danni, he could have been anybody, some crackpot or something.'

'It wasn't quite like that, Dallas.' Danni felt her anger start to flare. Really, Dallas could be so possessive at times she felt stifled. 'Besides, he was a friend of Rick's,' she added as she drew the car to a halt in front of the house.

'He still could have been anybody. Look, Danni, I'm sorry.' Dallas sighed. 'I didn't mean to put you through an inquisition. I just worry about you. Put it down to old-fashioned jealousy,' he remarked, climbing out of the car.

'Coming in for a cup of tea, Dallas?' asked Danni's father, who had walked out on to the verandah as they pulled up in front of the house. Jock Mathieson was a stockily built man, grey-haired with leathery skin weathered by his years spent under the relentless Australian sun.

'No, thanks, Jock.' Dallas stifled a yawn. 'I want to ring a couple of friends to let them know how Danni fared and then I think I'll hit the sack early tonight. All that fresh air plus the excitement have taken their toll.'

'Okay, then,' replied Jock, going inside, 'see you in the morning.'

'After today's effort I have a feeling you're going to take the racing world by storm,' Dallas grinned sheepishly at Danni, changing the subject after Jock's interruption.

'I don't know about the world,' she said drily, thankful to have the conversation back to more mundane topics. 'Let's just take it a race at a time. But thanks for everything and sorry we couldn't win. 'Night, Dallas.'

Dallas gave her the thumbs up sign before striding across to his small flat in the men's quarters.

Slowly, Danni followed her father into the house, a frown puckering her forehead. It was already seven-forty. That gave her twenty minutes to wait for Shiloh to call. 'I'm going to take a quick shower, Pop, then I'll tell you all about the races. Won't be long.'

'Right, love. I'll put the kettle on.' Her father's voice came from the kitchen.

'The car went like a dream, Pop,' Danni gaily told her father a quarter of an hour later. 'I think I have a better than even chance of doing well in this series.'

His daughter didn't notice the slight stiffening of her father's smile. He appeared about to make a comment, then decided against it and hugged his daughter's slight figure against him before he set her cup of tea on the table and sat down opposite her. They chatted amicably for a while until Jock stood up to rinse his cup under the tap and set it on the sink to drain. He turned back to his daughter when the ringing of the telephone cut through the air.

Danni froze in her seat, her heart in her mouth as her father innocently reached around the corner and picked up the receiver. 'She's a bit early, isn't she? Any problems, Paul?' her father asked his young manager, and listened intently to the other man for a few moments. 'Okay, lad, I'll leave it to you. If you need me down there just give me a call.'

He replaced the receiver. 'One of the mares is foaling early, but Paul can't see any complications.' He looked at his daughter and frowned in concern at the paleness of her face. 'What is it, love? Don't you feel well?' He put his arm around her shoulders in concern.

'I'm all right, Pop. The phone just gave me a fright, that's all.' Danni pulled herself together with an effort, waves of disappointment still washing over her.

Jock gave her a direct look and sat back down opposite her. 'What's the real trouble, love? Now that I think about it you've been jumpy all night, ever since we sat down here an hour ago.'

'Must be reaction after the excitement of the day.' Her laugh didn't even sound convincing to her own ears and at the penetrating look on her father's face she ran a shaky hand over her eyes. 'It's nothing earth-shattering, Pop, really. I was expecting a phone call and I thought that might have been it. It gave me a bit of a fright.'

'Mmm.' Her father looked thoughtfully at her. 'This phone call, was it an important one?'

'Oh, not really,' she said nonchalantly, and felt herself blush. Liar! said an inner voice.

Her father's eyes twinkled. 'A masculine or feminine caller?'

'Pop, you're beginning to sound like a television panel game! Your next question should be "Is it vegetable or mineral?"'

Jock chuckled. 'Judging by your cagey non-reply I'd take a guess at masculine.'

She looked at her father and laughed reluctantly. 'Yes, it's masculine.'

'I've never seen you this uptight about a young fellow before.' His face had sobered. 'Do I know him, by any chance?'

Danni hesitated, undecided about mentioning Shiloh O'Rourke at this early state. It was too new, too fragile, too intense to be put into words.

'Danni!' Dallas's voice called as his footsteps crossed the verandah.

'In the kitchen,' called Danni's father. 'What's the trouble?' he asked as Dallas strode purposefully into the room, his face set.

'I've just been talking on the phone to a mate of mine and I asked him if he knew of anyone in the racing game called Shiloh. All he could come up with was Shiloh O'Rourke.'

'Shiloh O'Rourke!' exclaimed Jock, his face paling as he seemed to slump back in his chair. 'What's this all about, Dallas?'

'You'll have to ask Danni,' said Dallas, standing with his legs apart and his hands on his hips. 'Did that fellow you met on the practice track call himself Shiloh O'Rourke?'

Danni looked from Dallas's set face to her father's shocked one, a quiver of dread turning her legs to jelly. 'He . . . that's who he was. Shiloh O'Rourke.' She paused. 'Pop, what's the matter? He said he was a friend of Rick's. Do you . . . do you know him?'

'Friend? Hah!' ejaculated Dallas.

Her father wiped a shaky hand across his eyes and nodded slowly. 'He knew Rick. They'd known each other for years. They used to call him Rourkey. He was competing in the same race that day at Sandown and he crashed when Rick did.' Jock sighed. 'His legs were pretty badly smashed up and I heard he wouldn't walk again.'

'That's not all, Danni,' said Dallas, like a hawk coming in for the kill. 'Everyone holds him responsible for the crash, and for the deaths of Rick and young Don Christie.'

Danni appealed to her father as he sat stiffly in his chair. Her heart seemed to jump in her breast and then constricted painfully. 'Pop, please! Say it's not true!'

The flashes of memories materialised out of the mist at the back of Danni's mind. It was as though a curtain had been raised and little pieces began to tumble down into place. Shiloh hadn't wanted her to question him about the past, about racing. He always managed to deftly steer her away from anything touching on the subject. That day on the practice track. At the restaurant. Her head was spinning.

. If Rick had mentioned anyone called Rourkey at all in the early days she couldn't recall it. 'But . . .' Her lips were stiff with shock. 'How can he be to blame, Pop? You never said . . . I thought it was a clear-cut accident?'

Shiloh's fair good looks and smiling face swam before her, quickly followed by the wariness in his expression on the odd occasions when he spoke of his association with Rick and motor racing in general. Now she recalled with absolute clarity how often he had actually turned the conversation away from those subjects during the night they went out to dinner.

Her father still sat pale and tense.

'Humph!' Dallas was looking disgusted. 'An accident? Careless driving, more likely. It was only good luck on O'Rourke's part that the significant section of the videotape was damaged so no charges could be laid.'

Jock Mathieson stirred and motioned Dallas to a chair. 'You'd better sit down,' he said tiredly, and turned to Danni. 'Maybe I should have told you the whole story, love, but I just didn't see the need to upset you any more than was necessary. And I just never thought to see or hear of Rourkey again.'

'He should have been jailed for manslaughter as far as I'm concerned.' Dallas sat down angrily. 'The nerve of the guy, even coming near here, let alone making himself known to Danni.' He hit one fist into his palm. 'Any other day I'd have been out at the practice track with her and I would have sent him on his way, believe me. I don't know how he can have the gall to face people!'

'I don't suppose there's any mistake it was him?' asked Jock.

'No, I don't think so.' Dallas shook his head, his face flushed with suppressed anger. 'He came out of hospital in Sydney about five weeks ago. My mate tells me he's also heard a rumour that O'Rourke wants to get back into racing. Formula 5000's. Anyone who'd take him on would need his head read,' Dallas finished disdainfully.

'For heaven's sake, will you two stop talking as though I'm not here!' Danni turned to her father imploringly. 'I think you'd better tell me, Pop,' she said quietly. 'I have a right to know.'

Jock nodded his head sadly. 'Make us another cuppa first, will you, love?' He sighed and rubbed a gnarled hand over his face. 'In the old days I had a lot of time for Rourkey, although I hadn't seen him in years. Neither had Rick. He spent a lot of time racing in the U.K. I think he was working over there—before he came back here to Formula 5000's. That race at Sandown was his first since his return to the Aussie scene.'

'He should have taken the advice given to him,' Dallas butted in. 'Everyone told him he should build up to that race by entering some of the lesser races.' He looked at Danni. 'Did he say why he had the cheek to call in here?' he asked aggressively.

Danni shook her head. 'He said he was just driving past and he saw my Lola on the track.'

'God, he's got some nerve!' Dallas spluttered. 'I wouldn't have been able to show my face.'

'Dallas, just tell me what happened.' Danni turned to him.

'Yes, you'd better tell her, Dallas,' Jock said quietly.

'I remember I didn't get down to Sandown that weekend because my father was taken ill,' he began, 'but my mates told me all about it later. It was a great day for racing weatherwise, one of the best. They said Don Christie was the fastest qualifier but only a split second faster than Rick. They were on the first grid. O'Rourke was back on the fourth, wasn't he, Jock?'

Danni's father nodded. 'He was racing his own car. He had a couple of independent sponsors, but I think he mostly financed himself.'

'O'Rourke drove like a maniac,' Dallas continued.

'Now, hold on, Dallas. Let's try to be rational.' Jock waved a hand. 'There was nothing wrong with Rourkey's driving before the accident. He drove outstandingly well and made up three or four position in half a dozen laps.'

'That remains to be seen,' remarked Dallas. 'When he did get to the front he was going to stay there by fair means or foul. Don Christie and Lex Grant went to take him on the bend and O'Rourke braked too sharply, probably lost his nerve, and that was that.'

'We've no proof that he lost his nerve, Dallas,' Jock said softly. 'He simply made a mistake and, God knows, living with that on his conscience ever since can't have been overly pleasant.' He turned back to Danni. 'Rourkey ended up pinned in his car where he crashed into the fence. They said it took the rescue team ten minutes to cut him out of his car,' Jock said flatly. 'Rick and young Christie spun into each other. They ... they didn't stand a chance.'

Danni could almost hear the crowd, smell the familiar odour of petrol and oil and hot tyres, feel the excitement of the race, with the crowd roaring and surging to its feet, anticipating further tussles as the three jockeyed for the lead. Then would have come that fatal moment as a mêlée of cars came together in a horrific rending of metal and shatter of fibreglass.

In her mind's eye Danni could picture the whole scene, the smoking, twisted cars, the rescue crews in action assisted by the firefighters and ambulancemen as they worked frantically to free the drivers, the flag marshals waving two yellow flags to warn the other competitors that the track was completely blocked, and the stunned, shuffling silence of the crowd, watching on in horror.

She closed her eyes, a lump rising in her throat, trying not to think about Rick or ...

'I'm sorry, love. I didn't want to have you know the details,' Jock said quietly.

'All the newspaper reports said it was O'Rourke's fault. I reckon he should have been jailed, and so does everyone in the racing game,' barked Dallas. 'He's a Jonah. Even his girl-friend dropped him like a hot brick. I don't remember her name, but she was pretty well known. A model or something.'

'The Board of Enquiry thought Don Christie's inside front tyre blew on the corner,' began Jock.

'Rubbish, Jock! O'Rourke misjudged and braked and couldn't pull his car out of it,' exclaimed Dallas.

'What's the use?' Jock's voice was flat. 'Nothing and no one can judge what happened. A thousand enquiries won't bring Rick or young Christie back.'

'Oh, Pop!' Danni put her arm around her father's shoulders.

He patted her arm. 'There's nothing to be gained by getting upset, love,' he tried to smile, and sighed. 'I take it you liked Rourkey well enough,' he remarked.

'I ... Oh, Pop! It was his call I was expecting this evening. I went out to dinner with him on Thursday night and we had such a nice time,' said Danni, forgetting for a moment Dallas's presence.

'Dinner?' Dallas's face turned impossibly redder. 'You don't mean to say ... you went out with O'Rourke?' he asked her in part anger, part disbelief.

'I ... he asked me. It was a spur-of-the-moment thing. I was going to ask him about ... about Rick.' Her voice caught. 'We didn't ... we didn't get around to it.'

Of course she couldn't mention, dared not even think of those burning kisses and caresses they had shared, but the fleeting memory of them brought the colour to her pale cheeks. She somehow felt now that she had betrayed them all, been taken in by the enemy. 'I wish now I'd never met him,' she said angrily.

She tried to keep Shiloh's long thin face from her mind as a question kept churning in her mind. How much did she care? Those words hammered in her brain while the answer eluded her. Her father was so right. Nothing could bring Rick back, but if Shiloh O'Rourke was responsible for Rick's death then he should be made to pay for it.

CHAPTER FIVE

On Monday morning, after rising early from her sleepless night, Danni drove her little red sedan along the highway on her way to work. Life had a habit of going callously onwards no matter how much pain had to be endured.

Shiloh O'Rourke. Her lips twisted cynically. Since his advent on Saturday afternoon it seemed that her thoughts had seldom been free of him. Now her mind was in a turmoil over the whole situation.

She found herself trying to convince herself that she disliked him, disliked the way his eyes moved boldly over her, causing her heartbeat to accelerate, her breathing to become irregular. And after the revelations of the previous night it should be so easy to dislike him intensely. All at once, without warning, she was recalling the sensations she experienced as his hands moved over her, following the trail burned by his eyes. Her skin tingled at the thought, her lips parting in anticipation.

These fantasies only served to fan the spark of her anger and hurt. She recognised that it hurt, and it was a feeling of hurt that ran deep within her. She couldn't deny the spark of attraction that burned between them. It was there no matter how much she wanted to deny its existence, and she could only be thankful that she had learned of his involvement in that fateful race before she had become more deeply involved with him. And that she could have lost her head over him she admitted to herself as she drove across the Currumbin bridge with the early morning traffic.

A shaft of pain twisted inside her, the pain of loss and disillusionment. Why hadn't he been honest with her from the beginning so that she wouldn't have to hear it from Dallas and her father? That was what hurt the most. While a small voice inside her asked, in all fairness, how she expected him to have broached the subject.

His face swam before her. He wasn't handsome, but then again, she had to admit that he was far from unsightly. His jaw was square and his chin firm, with character. Character? Her lips twisted. The creases in either cheek gave her the impression that he was always smiling, and the way the corners of his mouth lifted upwards only added to this impression. His eyes were his most arresting feature, she felt, due mainly to their unusual colour, light brown flecked with yellow-orange and fringed by thick almost fair lashes which matched his curved fair eyebrows. She suspected his hair would bleach to almost white if he spent any time at all in the sun. If the hollows beneath his cheekbones, which were apparently due to his prolonged stay in hospital, were filled out, he could be quite startlingly attractive.

The toot of an impatient horn of the car behind her brought Danni's mind back out of her reverie and she pulled her thoughts up as she drove away from the already changed green light. She could cause an accident herself if she didn't keep her mind on what she was doing.

Uninvited, the memory of the moment Shiloh had left her on Thursday night came vividly back to her, reminding her of the sensation of pure physical awareness that he evoked in her and her reluctance to see him leave. Had he wanted to stay that night she didn't think she would have had the strength to deny him, and her cheeks burned now at her weakness.

Thank goodness he hadn't phoned last night. She knew she wouldn't have been able to speak to him. Her throat would have closed on her. And she still had that call to face, because she knew he would call eventually.

For two days Danni lived in dread of Shiloh's phone call. She kept herself busy, knowing if she allowed herself to dwell on it at all, she would go steadily mad. She stayed chatting to Lisa at her flat until late on Monday evening and on Tuesday evening she was in two minds as to whether she should go out or stay home.

Eventually she decided on the latter and began to add the newspaper clippings about last weekend's races to her scrapbook. She had started the scrapbook last year and it was nearly a third full of photographs and reports on the races she had competed in previously, races which had led up to her acceptance as a competitor in the Driver to Europe series.

She was glancing idly through the earlier pages, checking the times she had made, when the telephone jangled loudly in the hall. A couple of seconds elapsed before she could move, before she got to her feet and walked slowly into the hall. It had to be Shiloh, she told herself resignedly, and took a deep steadying breath before lifting the receiver.

'Hello. Danni Mathieson speaking,' she said calmly. At last she could get it over and done with, remove the time bomb she had been living with since Sunday.

'Hello, Danni.' His familiar deep voice, sounding deeper on the telephone, had her reaching for the telephone stool before her shaking legs gave way beneath her. How could he possibly have done what they said? How could he have been so careless, so negligent? How could he have caused such havoc?

'Danni?'

'Yes, I'm here. How . . . how are you, Shiloh?' she stammered, wishing she could control the tremble in her voice even if her body responded involuntarily to his smooth tone.

'Fine.' His voice was smiling, caressing. 'I'm sorry I didn't ring you. I was tied up all weekend, until after eleven on Sunday night, and I thought you'd most probably be in bed by then.'

'Yes. Yes, I was,' was all she could say, and she forced a deliberate coolness into her tone.

'I believe you had a successful day on Sunday. Congratulations. I'm sorry I missed it.'

'Thank you. It was better than I'd hoped for and the car went superbly. How did you know?' she asked, and then realised he probably read the newspapers just like everyone else.

'Nathan rang me on Monday,' he laughed. 'As a matter of fact he gave me a blow-by-blow account of the events, right down to the last puff of exhaust smoke. Thanks for taking him under your wing, Danni. He's quite taken with you, if I read the signs rightly. Perhaps I'll have to look to my laurels.'

'Nathan's a nice boy. I like him,' she said carefully.

There was an infinitesimal pause.

'Ah, yes. Well, I'm still in Sydney, but I hope to

be home some time on Friday. I'll call to see you on Friday evening. Are you working late?'

Danni steeled herself. 'No, I finish early, but I can't say if I'll be home on Friday evening. I may be going out.'

'Just may be?' His voice had stopped smiling. 'I'd appreciate it if you could be home when I call. Where were you going?'

'Er—to a cabaret with some friends from the raceway,' she replied evenly.

'Do you have to go?' he asked.

'Well, I said I would,' she said, bending the truth a little. The cabaret was being held on Friday night, but she hadn't intended going.

Shiloh began to say something when he was interrupted by noises in the background, voices laughing, as though a door had been opened. At least one of the voices was female. 'Darling, hurry up with your silly old call. We're waiting!' The silky words drifted faintly along the line.

'Danni? I have to ring off now. I'll be there on Friday night. I particularly want to talk to you, so I'll see you then.'

She went to tell him not to call, but he had broken the connection.

Danni replaced the receiver and walked back into the living-room. So he wanted to talk to her and she was to be there waiting. He could jolly well go and take a long walk off a short jetty! She would definitely go to the cabaret and Shiloh would make a wasted journey. That should give him the message. She forced aside a tiny feeling of cowardice. As far as she was concerned he could stay in Sydney and she wouldn't be sorry. And the owner of the sultry voice was welcome to him!

She walked across to her stereo unit and selected a record at random, setting it on the turntable and adjusting the volume before settling back in a comfortable chair.

It wasn't until one particular song broke through her troubled thoughts that she realised she had unconsciously chosen 'Hot August Night'. As the fullness of Neil Diamond's voice flowed over her Danni felt the tears begin to fall. 'Shiloh, you always came . . .'

She sobbed long after the record had finished. She was unable to stop. She tried to believe that she only cried for the brother she had loved so much, but, deep down, she knew part of her mourned the loss of someone else who had been about to become so important to her, someone tall and thin with unruly waving fair hair. Someone who would always stand before her bathed in the shadow of her brother's untimely death.

To say that Dallas was surprised to receive a phone call from Danni inviting him to go along with her to the cabaret was an understatement. Since he had dropped his bombshell about Shiloh O'Rourke on Sunday night he had cursed himself for all kinds of a fool. The look on Danni's face had told him that she was more involved with the fellow than he had suspected and he had been sure that she would hold against him the fact that he had been the one to tell her of O'Rourke's true colours. When she phoned he jumped at the chance of taking her out. He would have followed her barefoot along the Birdsville Track, he told himself.

Thus, on Friday evening, Danni sat on tenterhooks waiting for Dallas's arrival. She wanted to be a long time gone when Shiloh arrived. Standing up, she paced to the window for the tenth time, gazing anxiously along the street.

You'll have to face him some time, reminded an inner voice. Yes, but not tonight. She wasn't ready. She didn't feel she had herself together enough for the encounter, for that was how she looked upon it, as an encounter. And she knew that undoubtedly Shiloh O'Rourke would be a formidable opponent in any altercation. So what if delaying the skirmish was cowardly? She couldn't help that. Tonight she felt cowardly. Maybe tomorrow, next week, she would be ready. Ha! exclaimed that same inner voice, very reminiscent of her conscience.

At that moment Dallas drove up and Danni closed her mind to the whole thing as she dashed down to greet him. She felt a small pang of compunction as his eyes lit up at her enthusiastic welcome, but she was determined to enjoy herself at the cabaret.

It was well after midnight when Dallas delivered her home, and he was decidedly pleased with himself and the evening. Danni had been her usual gay self, shining in the large hall with the glow of enjoyment, and he had been justifiably proud to be sitting and dancing with her. That he had successfully deterred one or two other hopeful young men who gravitated in Danni's direction only added to his self-satisfaction.

He glanced sideways at her. To Dallas, Danni Mathieson was the epitome of his kind of girl. She was attractive, vivacious, and goodnatured. She was a more accomplished driver than he had ever hoped to be, and this filled him with the utmost admiration and not the slightest spark of envy.

He noticed that she was a trifle subdued now that

they were nearly home, but he put that down to tiredness. After all, they had danced every dance. He drew the car to a halt in front of Danni's house, and her heart sank as he switched off the engine and pulled her towards him. Holding her gently in his arms, he kissed her lightly on the lips, almost as though he expected her to pull back.

'It was a fantastic night, wasn't it?' he asked, keeping her lightly in the circle of his arms. 'I haven't had such a beaut evening in ages.'

'Yes, it was very nice. Great fun,' Danni replied, unconsciously comparing Dallas with Shiloh. She forcibly pushed from her mind the memories of the time she had spent in Shiloh's arms in this very spot just eight days ago and the devastating effect he had had on her senses. She had to stop herself pushing Dallas's hands away in revulsion and she remained stiffly guilty in his arms.

'Mm, so are you very nice,' murmured Dallas, moving closer. 'I like your perfume.' He put his lips to her temple.

'Dallas, I'm rather tired and I have to go to work in the morning,' she began, and he sighed.

'Yes, I know. But you're so beautiful, Danni,' he pulled her close against his chest with more than his usual force. 'Danni, you know how I feel about you.'

Danni gently pushed a hand against him. 'Please, Dallas. We've been through all that. I . . .'

'I know, I know. Good friends.' He grimaced and then moved reluctantly away. 'But I'll wear you down yet, you'll see. I can wait.'

'Maybe.' Danni smiled, relieved. 'Anyway, thanks for taking me.' She climbed out of the car and hurried along the path to the door, unconsciously expecting Shiloh to pounce from behind each bush.

Dallas waited until she had the foyer light on before switching on his ignition and lights and making a U-turn in the street. He drove off with a quick beep of his horn.

Danni barely heard it. Her breath had caught in her throat. Had that been a green sedan parked along the street on the opposite side of the road caught for a split second in Dallas's headlights? She peered into the darkness, but it was past the street light and she wasn't able to decide whether she had imagined it or not. It was probably her imagination. She had only seen it because she had expected to see it.

She hurried inside and locked the door, sliding the chain across, sighing thankfully. Why was she getting so uptight? There were plenty of green cars around and if there was a car parked in the street it didn't have to be a Lotus. She was just being super-sensitive tonight. He would have been and gone.

What had he thought when he arrived to find that she hadn't waited for him? He would have been angry, to say the least, but after all, she had told him not to come. If he chose to ignore that then it was his own lookout. Well, it was done. There was no going back.

Yawning sleepily, tired from her emotion-charged evening, Danni slipped into the bathroom for a quick shower. During the entire evening she had lived on her nerves, laughing and joking, dancing. To all outward appearances she had been having a ball. Little did everyone know that she was being driven by an urge to cover her guilty conscience, all the while living in dread of Shiloh walking into the middle of the cabaret and forcibly removing her, although she knew he would have no possible way of knowing she was there.

Pushing thoughts of Shiloh O'Rourke to the back of her mind, she slipped a cool floral cotton nightie over her head. It reached almost midway down her thighs and was held up by two thin straps tied on her shoulders. She was walking from the bathroom to her bedroom in her bare feet when a controlled knock on the front door nearly frightened her out of her wits. Her heart leapt into her mouth and she stood poised, unable to move.

'Danni! Open the door, please.' His voice came evenly through the wooden panels. 'Danni, I know you're there. Open the door!' he said a little louder.

'It's late. I'm ... I'm going to bed,' she began.

'Danni, if you don't open this door I'm going to break the bloody thing in,' he said softly, in a tone more frightening for its quietness.

'Please, Shiloh, go away. I don't want to see you. You'll wake the neighbours,' she appealed to him.

'One minute, Danni, then I bust the door. The noise will surely give the neighbours food for speculation for months. Please yourself. Do I come in quietly or with a flourish?' he asked expressionlessly.

'All right. Just a minute, I ... I'm not dressed.' She ran across the living-room and into her bedroom, grabbing her cotton brunch coat from her bed, pulling the door to behind her as she slipped the brunch coat over her short nightie.

She moved slowly to the door and, checking that the chain was secure, she unlocked the catch and opened the door a couple of inches.

He was standing on the landing, and in the shaft of light from inside that gleamed through the open door his appearance didn't fill her with reassurance. He looked dishevelled. His shirt was unbuttoned and fell open at the neck and he had obviously been running his hands through his hair.

But it was the rigidness in his stance and the intensity of the expression on his face that caused her to draw her breath in a quiver of fear. There was tension in every part of his body, in his long legs, thrust slightly apart, in the hands shoved into the pockets of his slacks and in the hard aggression of his jaw.

'Please, go away, Shiloh. It's late and I'm too tired to talk,' Danni began in an attempt at firmness. Perhaps if she showed him she was unintimidated by him he would leave.

'I know it's late.' His voice snapped out between his clenched teeth. 'Believe me, I know just how late it is. I've been sitting in my car since eight o'clock and I know every damn minute that's dragged past. I'm tired. I'm stiff. And I'm bloody thirsty, so for a start, you could offer me a drink.'

'I'll ... I'll get you a glass of water.' Danni went to close the door.

'Danni, if you don't open that door I'll ...' He raised his voice and his eyes flashed in the darkness, yellow and tawny, like a tiger stalking in the night. 'And don't think that paltry little chain will stop me. Those things are designed to keep honest people out.'

'Oh, all right. Keep your voice down.' She slid the chain off its hook and opened the door. 'But you'll have to go when you've had your drink. I was just about to go to bed.'

His eyes moved over her short brunch coat and bare feet, his look causing her mouth to dry and her heartbeat to falter, before he strode past her into the hall and through to the living-room.

'What would you like to drink?' she asked, moving to a small bar in the corner of the room. 'There's not much variety, I'm afraid. I ... Pop and I, we don't drink much.'

'Scotch?'

She nodded and poured him a small measure. 'Do you want anything with it?'

Shiloh shook his head and disposed of the drink in one gulp. 'Aren't you going to join me in another?' he asked, setting the glass near the bottle, as he raised one fair eyebrow.

'No. No, thanks.' Danni poured him another smaller measure and pointedly put the bottle away.

He grimaced, and taking the glass, strode across the living-room and stood with his back to her, examining a framed print on the wall.

Danni remained behind the bar, feeling the need to keep something solid between them.

'I came here straight from the airport. Needless to say I was decidedly angry to find you were absent,' he said quietly, his back still to her.

'Well, I'm sorry you came along for nothing, but I did warn you I'd be out,' she replied defiantly.

There was a brief silence.

'Who was the guy who so gallantly escorted you home and bade you such a romantic goodnight?' he asked sarcastically.

'It was Dallas Byrne, a good friend of mine,' Danni retorted, feeling inexplicably guilty and subsequently angry. 'Although I don't know that it's any business of yours.'

He pivoted on his heel, downing the remainder of his Scotch and walking across towards her. Danni's heart fluttered like a trapped bird, but he just set his empty glass deliberately on the bar top and, resting his hands there, leant easily on them, smiling humourlessly.

'Ah, yes, the redoubtable Dallas Byrne,' he said drily. 'Your mechanic, I believe.'

'Yes, he is. And a very good one, too. Just about the best.' She lifted her chin.

'He seemed to enjoy a lengthy goodnight. Is he as good at making love as he is with cars?' he asked levelly, his eyes burning into hers.

Danni stared at him, her blue eyes wide, locked in his mocking stare, and she was almost hypnotised by the sparkling brightness of his cat's eyes. He was playing with her before he pounced, just like a predatory cat.

She forced her lips to move. 'Dallas is a friend. That's all you need to know. How intimate our friendship is, is a private thing between Dallas and myself.' For a split second she thought she had gone too far, but Shiloh remained where he was, his knuckles growing white on the bar top.

'No matter,' he bit off, turning away abruptly and thrusting his hands deep into his pockets. 'We'll leave it, for the moment. May I ask you why you felt you had to evade me this evening? I mean, I suppose you do have a reason. When I left last week I went with the apparently mistaken impression that you could barely wait until I returned.' He swung around again to face her. 'Now, Danni, how could I have been so wrong?' he asked with sarcasm.

She watched him, suddenly frightened by his

steely control. She was trapped behind the bar and at his mercy. Slowly, carefully, she moved from behind the bench top and stood by the opening. At least from there she could make a dash for the door.

All at once he was unfamiliar to her, a stranger, a cold quiet stranger. His fair good looks, his dancing eyes, that smiling mouth, they were all gone. In their place were features etched in steel, eyes brightly cold, long face tightly covering a suppressed anger, almost frustration, and his mouth, a mouth that had once moved so devastatingly on her in gentleness and burning reciprocated mounting passion, was now thin and cold, clamped in tight control.

He was still waiting for an answer to his question and she nervously shrugged her shoulders, striving to hold on to the slim thread of her own control. 'You . . . you must have misunderstood,' she said, not meeting his eyes.

'Oh, I see. I misunderstood. How simple.' He paced about the living-room like a caged tiger. 'Tell me, do you indulge yourself in these passion-packed interludes very often?'

'It's a modern world.' She tried to laugh and didn't quite pull it off.

Shiloh's eyes raked her still form and she lifted her chin to bolster her courage which was slipping away from her with every passing moment.

He paced about a little more. 'This Dallas Byrne, I guess he's fairly familiar with the racing scene? And I suppose,' he turned to watch her expression carefully, 'he's also familiar with my illustrious career?'

Danni's face suffused with colour and he made a sound as though he had expelled a breath he had been holding inside for some time.

'I suspected as much,' he said flatly. 'Nathan said he didn't tell you, so it had to be Dallas Byrne or your father.'

'Why didn't you tell me yourself?' The question burst from Danni before she could hold it back.

The anger that had held him rigid before seemed to have drained out of him and all that remained was a cold cynicism that twisted in a vulnerable spot somewhere deep inside Danni's heart. But she steeled herself against it. She reminded herself that, in all probability, he had been responsible for the death of her brother, her own flesh and blood, and a lethal anger kindled within her, and burned, wanting to erupt and cascade her hurt upon him.

'Could you see me dropping it all into the conversation as we sat over dinner?' he asked flatly. 'Oh, by the way, I was somewhat involved in the accident that killed your brother. More wine?' he mimicked bitterly.

Danni flinched. She wanted to spring on him, flay him with her hands, her fingernails, relieve some of her pent-up frustrations, her desire for revenge, her anger, her uncertainties about the whole thing. But she stood as stiffly as he did and watched his face. 'And did you kill my brother?'

CHAPTER SIX

THE look on Shiloh's face made her catch her breath, but she stood her ground as he strode across until he was standing right in front of her, his hands clenched at his sides.

'I've faced one official enquiry, been proved innocent. I've faced a hundred, a thousand, other personal enquiries since then and I have been found guilty without a shred of concrete evidence to point to my guilt and, all in all, I'm heartily sick and tired of putting my case to the people. Not that those people count.'

In his eyes Danni thought she caught a flash of pain, but it was gone before she could be certain.

'There are winners and there are losers, Danni, and it was your brother's turn to lose. I survived and I'm going to go on surviving.'

'Until your turn comes around? That's very impressive. But you still haven't answered my question. Were you responsible?' Danni felt an outward calmness while her heartbeat echoed so loudly in her head she thought he must hear it.

Suddenly his control snapped. His strong fingers bit into the flesh of her bare arms and he shook her until she was dizzy and cried out at the pain he was inflicting.

'God, I could so easily squeeze the life out of you without any compunction,' he said hoarsely, his eyes burning as his hands moved to circle her throat.

Hot tears spilled over her lashes and coursed down her cheeks.

'And you can cut the feminine tears,' he added cruelly, 'because the way I feel at the moment nothing is going to appeal to my better nature.'

His hands hauled her against him and his lips closed over hers in fierce, almost desperate possession, grinding her lips against her teeth until she tasted her own blood. She was powerless to move from his punishing hold and with a stab of panic she realised his anger had given way to desperate driving passion and she began to struggle against his vice-like grip. She wrenched her head to the side, away from his punishing mouth. His lips surrendered hers, only to slide downward to the base of her throat, to plunder there.

She could feel Shiloh trembling and her fear intensified. Her brunch coat fell to the floor and his hands seared through the thin material of her nightdress. Realising she was no match for his superior strength, in desperation she trod sharply on his foot and pushed herself backwards with all the power she could muster.

Shiloh gasped in shock more than pain, but his hold only slackened slightly so that they overbalanced, still locked together. At the last minute Shiloh instinctively put out his hand to save them as they fell against the door of Danni's bedroom. His hand hit the door with some force and would most probably have stopped their fall but for the fact that the door was not closed properly, and it swung open under the impact of the weight of their bodies to burst back against the wall with a resounding crash.

The door only momentarily impeded their fall and Shiloh spun himself around to cushion Danni's fall, so that Danni would go down on top of him. They came up against Danni's bed with a thud and Shiloh's gasp of pain seemed to echo about the walls of Danni's room.

They had fallen in an untidy heap on the bed and Danni quickly struggled to her feet, expecting Shiloh's arms to reach for her again, but she stood alone beside the bed, her breast heaving. With shaking hands she clutched the strap of her nightdress which had snapped in their fall. She became aware that Shiloh's breathing was laboured with pain and that he hadn't moved from where he had fallen. She felt for the switch of her reading lamp at the top of her bed and flicked it on.

What she saw filled her with horror. Even in the dim circle of light she could see that his face was deathly grey and that beads of perspiration glistened on his brow. He was lying stiffly, dragging breaths in the shallow careful gasps of someone who has experienced excruciating pain, pain that causes the terror of its pending return.

'Shiloh,' she whispered, putting a tentative hand on his arm. His muscles were rigid and only his eyes moved towards her. 'Shiloh, what is it?' Her voice trembled and she grabbed a handful of tissues from the box on her dressing table and gently wiped his brow.

He let out a long breath. 'My leg.' His voice was hoarse. 'I guess I fell on it, against the bed.'

'What can I do? Shall I get a doctor?' she asked.

'No, no. Just help me up so I can massage it.' He tried to raise himself on one elbow and grimaced with pain.

She pulled him back on to the bed, drawing the pillow down under his head. 'Lie still. I'll rub it for

you, just tell me how.' She gingerly lifted his legs on
to the bed so that he was lying flat. She went to pull
up the leg of his flared trousers so that she could
massage his leg properly and his hand took hold of
her arm.

'No, Danni, don't!'

She stopped and looked at him.

'My leg,' he said, 'it was fairly badly smashed up.
There's scars. It's not a pretty sight.'

'I've seen scars before, Shiloh. Now lie back.' She
gently removed his hand and proceeded to fold up
his trouser leg. Even knowing what to expect she
was unprepared for the criss-cross of deep etches that
ran the length of his leg from his knee. Her breath
caught, but she schooled her face before she turned
to look at him. His wry expression said 'I told you
so', but he made no comment as she began to massage
his leg from knee to ankle.

After a while he began to relax and some of the
tension went out of him.

'You should have left me to suffer,' he murmured
softly, 'after the way I behaved.'

Stopping to remove his shoes, she resumed her
gentle kneading. 'You're probably right,' she said
evenly.

Shiloh lapsed into silence again and some time
later she thought by his relaxed, even breathing
that he had fallen asleep. She'd have to leave
him here for the night and she'd use the spare
bedroom. She moved to turn off the bedside light,
leaning slightly over him to reach the switch. In
the dim light from the living-room she caught a
flash of tawny eyes as his hand fastened about her
wrist.

'Danni?' he said softly, and the word was almost a

caress. He exerted a slight pressure on her arm and pulled her on to the bed beside him. She landed softly against him, resting on his chest, and he gave a half sigh, half chuckle. 'You have a very soothing touch, Miss Mathieson. I don't suppose you'd consider a permanent position. The working conditions would be excellent and I promise not to beat you.' His words were sleepily sensual.

A sudden yearning to be held against him almost overwhelmed her, but she pushed herself away from him. 'Shiloh, this is insane . . .' she whispered, and he placed a silencing finger on her lips.

'Ssh! I thought you said it was late and you were tired. Besides,' he added huskily, 'you'll wake me up and then I might have my mind on other things.'

Danni's whole body flamed and she lay stiffly in his arms. He gave a sleepy chuckle and in no time he had drifted off into a relaxed sleep. She tried to hold her body away from his, but the whole evening's exertions began to take their toll. She remembered thinking she must get up and go into the spare bedroom, but she dropped off before she could make the move, her body moulding itself into the contours of his, his arms cradling her head on his shoulder.

Something disturbed Danni. She reluctantly began to fight off the desire to lapse back into a pleasant slumber. There had been a noise somewhere, a car door closing perhaps. And there was something heavy across her waist. She stirred sleepily, opening her eyes to the brightness of the morning. Her eyelids went to close in protest when her gaze fell on the pale blue shirt beneath her cheek. Her eyes opened widely and she moved her head, looking straight into a pair of tawny yellow ones which had opened at the same time hers did. Danni felt herself blush at the implications of their position and his lips twitched.

'I somehow feel you've ruined my reputation, Danni Mathieson.' His mouth was smiling, but his eyes were wary, almost cold, and watched her steadily.

'I've ruined your . . . why, you . . .' Danni tried to sit up, but his arms held her to him.

'I must apologise,' he said with that same smile. 'I have you in bed with me all night and I fall asleep. Inexcusable of me. I guess I'll have to try to restore my image before it cracks completely,' and his lips moved to cover hers.

Danni struggled to free herself, but his gently probing kisses, so different from those of the night before, were completely overruling her resolution. Her struggles became less frantic and ceased altogether, her hand slipping around his neck to move in the fine softness of his hair as she began to respond to the expertise of his kisses.

Shiloh turned on to his side until their bodies were pressed together, falling naturally into each other's contours, and his hands played sensuously along her spine. 'God, Danni, I've been just about out of my mind with wanting you,' he said huskily, his lips trailing over her eyelids and her jaw until they reclaimed her lips with a burning urgent intensity.

Danni responded with her own rising passion, drowning in the sensuousness of their embrace. Her mind told her that the bedroom was too intimate, that they were playing with fire, a burning, all-consuming fire that could very easily race out of hand.

Neither of them heard the key turn in the front door lock. They were too caught up in the sensations of the moment. They were unaware of the sound of footsteps in the hall, moving into the living-room, until a voice broke through the tension-filled world that had woven a cocoon of desire about them.

'You awake, Danni love? Whose is the flash green car blocking our driveway? I had to park out ...' Jock Mathieson's words faded away to nothing as he stared at his daughter through the open door of her bedroom.

Nothing was said for an immeasurable moment. The clock on Danni's bedside table ticked away innocently as the tension swelled. Then Jock turned away and leant on his hands on the bar top, his straight back to them.

Danni moved out of Shiloh's arms and ran into the living-room in horror. 'Pop! Pop, please—it's not what you think. Please believe me,' she cried, wondering if she could have said that in all honesty had her father appeared any later. 'I ... We ... Pop?' she appealed to his uncompromising back, her face aflame.

He turned slowly towards her, his eyes old and pain-filled. 'You're over twenty-one, Danni. I ... It's just a bit of a shock, that's all. I never thought my little girl ...'

'Pop, don't!' Danni flung her arms about her father, and for the first time felt him stiffen before his arms went slowly around her.

She heard Shiloh move into the room behind her and turned imploring eyes on him. His face was set and his eyes were guarded, absolutely expressionless.

'Jock,' he said, and her father's cold eyes didn't waver from the younger man's face as Danni felt his body grow more rigid.

'Pop, we can explain. You see, Shiloh and I ...' Her father moved away from her and walked across to the bar. He poured himself a glass of Scotch, and picking up her brunch coat from the untidy heap where it had fallen the night before he passed it wordlessly to her, his gaze not missing the broken strap of her nightdress.

'You'd better leave this to me, Danni.' Shiloh didn't look even slightly contrite or uncomfortable. 'My apologies, Jock. I'm afraid we didn't expect you.'

Danni watched as her father's features tensed and cringed inside. Something screamed inside her. Nothing between her father and herself would ever be the same again, and it was all Shiloh O'Rourke's fault. She turned on him. 'Oh, what's the use?' She was almost in tears. 'It can't be changed now. And you're only making it worse.' She turned back to her father. 'Pop, it was Shiloh's leg. He fell . . . he fell on it and I was massaging it for him and . . . and we fell asleep.' She raised her hands in frustration. 'That's all. Nothing else.'

Jock shrugged his shoulders with controlled anger, his eyes fixed on the glass in his hand.

Shiloh moved across to her, his limp more pronounced than she had noticed it before. 'Danni, be cool.' He put his arm around her so firmly that she couldn't shake it off. 'Jock, we're getting married. We'd like your blessing,' he said evenly, and Danni froze in shock.

Jock tossed down his drink.

'It seems to me you shouldn't wait around too long before you tie the knot,' he said flatly, pain in his eyes.

'Pop, don't listen to him! He's insane, I wouldn't marry him if . . .'

'Now, now, sweetie, that's not what you said last

night,' Shiloh smiled at her with his mouth.

'Why, you . . .' Danni stared at him stupefied.

'I'll leave you to argue it out,' said her father, 'I'm going to have a lie down before I fix up the downpipe that's leaking.' He walked across the hall to the bedroom he used when he was in town, closing the door firmly behind him.

Danni could feel that he couldn't bear to look at them and her heart constricted painfully. The restraint behind that even click of the door catch had her turning on Shiloh. He was standing against the bar, his foot on the rung of a bar stool, absently rubbing his leg.

'If you had any common decency at all you'd try to put things right with my father. But of course you haven't, have you?' She gave him a disdainful look as she went to go after her father, but Shiloh's voice stopped her.

'Leave him be for a moment, Danni. He needs breathing space.' He smiled crookedly at her. 'How about breakfast? Or am I to be chief cook and bottle washer this morning?'

'Breakfast? Oh, I could . . .!' She stamped her foot in frustration. 'You can get your own breakfast. In fact, you can starve for all I care. I'm going to take a shower and get dressed for work.' She headed across to the bedroom, turning determinedly away from their indentations in the bed. 'And you can stop with all this marriage bit, because it's not on. Things are bad enough as they are—no thanks to you!'

Twenty minutes later, dressed ready for her morning at the library, Danni hurried into the kitchen to make herself a quick piece of toast. She stopped in the kitchen doorway. Her place had been set neatly at the table and Shiloh turned from the stove with a plate on which rested a fluffy appetising omelette.

She sat down and looked at him. He wore a tea-towel tucked around his waist and when he'd set her plate in front of her he turned to pour her a cup of tea.

'Don't think I'm going to make a habit of this,' he said easily. 'I'll expect you to wait on me hand and foot when we're married.'

'We are not getting married,' Danni said flatly.

Their eyes met and duelled, and hers were the first to fall.

She sighed and, realising how hungry she was, began to eat. Anything so that she wouldn't have to look into those cold cat's eyes. How could she ever have thought them warm and gentle? The omelette was delicious, and as she had barely had any dinner the evening before owing to her nervousness she made short work of it.

Shiloh sat down opposite her, sipping his own tea.

'Aren't you having anything to eat?' she asked him ungraciously.

'This cup of tea will do for the present,' he said evenly.

'You know, you should eat properly or you'll never regain your strength,' she told him, trying to make easy conversation, wondering why she was bothering.

'Do I detect a note of concern?' he raised one cynical eyebrow.

Danni ignored that. 'You know you shouldn't joke about marriage. I just might call your bluff and accept your proposal.' She attempted a light laugh.

'I mean to marry you, Danni,' he said quietly, and her eyes flew to his face. She wasn't reassured by the determination in the steady coolness of his expression.

'I'd better go and see how Pop is.' She stood up. 'If you leave the dishes I'll wash them when I come home.'

'Leave your father to me. I'll talk to him before I leave,' he said.

Danni made no comment but marched along the hallway and tapped on her father's door. 'Pop, are you all right?'

The door opened and her father stood looking at both of them. 'I could do with a cuppa.'

'Shiloh's just made a pot so it will be nicely brewed for you. I have to go to work now. I ... will you be here at lunch time?'

He sighed. 'I'll be here, love,' he said, and opened his arms to her.

Danni flew into them and buried her face in her father's chest. 'Pop, I'm sorry!'

'I know, love. I didn't realise my little girl had grown into a woman, and it was quite a blow.' His eyes were still cold as they rested on Shiloh. 'But there'll be no more talk about marriage.'

'Pop, I'm . . .' she began.

'You'll be late, Danni,' Shiloh's voice came from the doorway.

She gave him a withering look. 'I'll see you later, Pop. And please don't worry.' She planted a kiss on his weathered cheek and went to walk coolly past Shiloh, but his arm came around her waist.

'Goodbye!' she said with feeling.

'I'll have to shift my car to let you out,' he said, planting an affectionate kiss on her cheek.

When she returned after work she was surprised to find Shiloh and her father in the middle of repairing the broken downpipe, and she went inside to prepare lunch. With her new plan spinning around in her mind she wanted a moment alone to mull it over.

She had spent the morning in something of a daze. Fortunately the library had not been busy and she had had plenty of time to think over the happenings of the previous night. Her cheeks burned every time she thought about spending the entire night in Shiloh's arms.

That Shiloh O'Rourke found her desirable she had no doubt, but as to marrying him—well, it was ludicrous. She'd rather marry Dallas Byrne! A comparison between the two men came unbidden to her mind, her response to Dallas compared to her response to Shiloh's shattering kisses, and she had the distinct feeling that she was kidding herself.

For the whole of the morning her mind spun about like a whirling dervish. She went from sensations of pure sensual delight at Shiloh's caresses to a burning horror that everyone, even her own father, believed him to be little better than a murderer. And she had allowed him to . . . Her own duplicity revolted her.

It was almost closing time when the fact that she knew so little about Shiloh O'Rourke was brought home to Danni again. She was tidying the library, clearing piles of books from the tables, straightening the newspapers and returning them to the newspaper racks. She picked up the Sydney paper and went to fold it neatly. The photo of Shiloh leapt out of the pulpy sheet and seemed to strike her between the eyes. She sank weakly on to a chair. Even the bad reproduction couldn't disguise the fact that it was him, or detract from his attractiveness, and Danni swallowed convulsively.

It was featured in the social section and Shiloh sat

beside a rather flashy blonde. Danni unfolded the paper so that she could read the caption beneath the photo: 'Snapped while dining at the Summit this week were the obviously fully recovered racing driver Shiloh O'Rourke and an old friend, the stunning Mrs Chris Damien. O'Rourke was severely injured in a pile-up of Formula 5000's at Sandown last year. We hear he may be taking to the track again soon, this time as part of the Chris Damien Racing Team. Mrs Damien is the former Model of the Year, Marla Warren.'

Danni stared at the words until they distorted beneath her gaze. How could Chris Damien even think of letting Shiloh drive for him? He had to replace Rick, she knew, but why did it have to be Shiloh who took his place?

A futile anger clutched at her, anger for Rick, and another less easily defined emotion, anger mixed with a totally new sensation, and in those first moments as she had stared transfixed at the photograph of Shiloh and the blonde girl she had known a burning jealousy. She grimaced. If Shiloh was so intent on marrying her he had a funny way of showing it. He didn't look like a man who wasn't enjoying himself. Her eyes went once again to the photograph, settling on Shiloh's attentive expression.

Maybe he had talked Chris Damien around through his wife. Hadn't Dallas said Shiloh had been involved with a model before the accident? The pieces fitted together too well. God, he was despicable! Her heart felt bruised and pain-filled and she bit back a rush of tears.

To think he had the audacity to ask her—no, to tell her she was marrying him! How could she possibly marry a man whose recklessness had led to her brother's death? And now he was stepping into Rick's place with Chris Damien.

Slowly Danni replaced the newspaper tidily over the stand and walked back to the desk. There should be more retribution here on earth. She had a burning desire to make him pay for his part in that crash. And so he deserved to pay, she told herself.

It was then that a plan began to form in her mind. It was all so simple. Shiloh desired her, wanted her— he had admitted as much. Hadn't he said just that this morning? She pushed memories of her own responses to the back of her mind. How would he feel if he married her and then discovered how much she hated him?

Yes, she'd marry him. For whatever reason he wanted her for his wife. And then, after the wedding, she'd take her revenge. He would be bound to a wife who spurned him, despised him. She quivered with excitement, and just a faint touch of apprehension. She'd hold him to that proposal, call his bluff. Oh, revenge would be so sweet!

Her father and Shiloh walked into the kitchen as she finished tossing the salad and the three of them sat down to the meal. The two men had obviously called an armed truce, spoke to each other warily, and if either of them noticed Danni was a little subdued no comment was made on the fact.

'Shiloh tells me you want to get married quietly next weekend,' Jock Mathieson gruffly dropped his bombshell as Danni was sipping her second cup of tea. Her eyes opened wide and her cup shook in her hand.

'If I said I was happy about this marriage I'd be lying,' he looked at his daughter, 'but Shiloh has convinced me that it's what you both want. Well, you're both adults . . .' he shrugged his shoulders. 'He was saying you wanted to go along to a register office. You know, your mother and I had a nice church wedding and—well, I always think a register office is sort of impersonal, and if you want to get married I won't have any hole-and-corner affair,' he finished firmly.

Danni took a deep breath, about to deny the haste for the ceremony. Next weekend? Shiloh must be mad! She glanced across at him, and he smiled that same cool enigmatic smile he seemed to have acquired in the last twenty-four hours.

'What your father is trying to say, sweetie,' he spoke before she had a chance to utter a word, 'is that he'd like us to get married out in the grounds at Mallaroo. And I told him that it sounded like a great idea, especially as we don't want to invite a large number of guests.'

Oh, how she'd like to knock his ego for six! He had it all planned, did he? Well, here comes the first chink in your wall, Shiloh O'Rourke!

'That would be a lovely idea,' she smiled guilelessly into his eyes and had the pleasure of seeing momentary shock register there. 'Now, why didn't we think of that, darling?' She put a finger to her cheek. 'Glory! If it's next Saturday we have lots of arrangements to make. I'll have to decide on a dress and we'll have to have a cake and decide who we'll invite.'

Apart from that one flicker of those yellow-brown eyes Shiloh had schooled his features and wasn't giving any of his reactions away via his facial expression.

'Perhaps you should leave it until the weekend after,' suggested her father.

'No. I'm going down south. I'm racing at Oran Park that weekend,' said Danni matter-of-factly, 'so it will have to be next Saturday or Saturday fortnight.'

'Racing?' her father repeated. 'But I thought if you were getting married you'd be giving motor racing away.'

Danni shook her head. 'Being married won't make any difference to my racing.' We won't be married that long, she added to herself. 'I've put too much effort into it, Pop, to give up now.' She looked pointedly at Shiloh, waiting for him to side with her father.

'Next Saturday fits in well for both of us, Jock,' he said decisively. 'There'll only be my immediate family on my side, my parents and young Nathan. And Bill Peterson. How about you, Danni?'

'Oh, just Lisa and Sue from the library,' she replied halfheartedly, suddenly feeling as though the whole thing had snowballed, had been taken out of her hands, and that she was lost somewhere in the middle, unable to stop herself in her headlong fall.

'Well, if it's all settled I'll get back out to Mallaroo right after lunch,' her father finished disgruntledly.

'I thought you'd stay for the weekend?' said Danni, with a decided reluctance about spending any time alone with Shiloh so soon.

'I did intend to, but Shiloh gave me a hand with the few odd jobs I had to do about the place, so I'm pleased I can get back to Mallaroo now. Paul and I are a little worried about one of the mares. I was half expecting a call from him this morning.'

'I'm taking Danni over to meet my parents this afternoon,' said Shiloh. 'They were somewhat surprised to hear that someone had eventually succeeded in tying me down.' He gave Danni a fond, teasing smile.

'Now, now, darling,' she said sweetly. 'You know it was you who wanted to do the tying down.'

'So long as you're both happy,' Jock innocently patted his daughter's hand. 'All I can ask is that you're as happy in your marriage as your mother and I were in ours.' But his eyes tiredly told her he thought she was making the mistake of her life.

CHAPTER SEVEN

IF the desire for retribution had burned brightly when the idea to marry him had first formed in her mind then it had grown into a raging inferno after she had made the acquaintance of Shiloh's parents. Shiloh's father had set the seal upon her scheme.

Shiloh drove her to his parents' Isle of Capri home after lunch so that they could relax and swim in the pool for the afternoon, and later she was to meet his parents on their return home. As Shiloh turned between the open wrought iron gates and up the short pebbled driveway Danni had received her first shock.

The house gleamed white, offset by the red-brown trim, and from the outside in the quiet cul-de-sac it appeared to be a modest Spanish-style home. However, as Shiloh stopped the car in front of a huge four-bay garage Danni realised that behind the simple high-walled fence was a veritable mansion. The hacienda ran through to the water, having its own mooring and boatshed. The O'Rourkes weren't exactly poverty-stricken, she thought, wryly.

Not bothering to unlock his garage door, Shiloh left the car parked where it was and without speaking they walked along a tiled pathway into the very attractive courtyard behind the garage. Similarly tiled, the courtyard had been beautifully landscaped with an ordered confusion of hanging plants, artistic rockeries and cascading greenery and, through an arch-

way, Danni could see a large turquoise blue swimming pool sparkling in the sunlight.

However, Shiloh opened a patterned glass sliding
door and waited for her to precede him into a large
family room. It housed a full-sized billiard table and
on the wall were racks of pool cues and other paraphernalia associated with the pastime. A Spanish
style bar, decorated with studded rich dark leather
and beaten copper motifs, continued in a curving
sweep from the family room into the living-room,
and the two rooms were separated by a huge double-
sided bookcase that stretched from floor to ceiling.

The living-room could only be described as subtly
magnificent. It rose two storeys with exposed dark
beams in the roof and an upstairs balcony ran along
one side, overlooking the room below. The stairs of
polished wood up to the top storey blended with the
rich cream of the carpet, the beige-toned wallpaper
and the deep chocolate lounge chairs.

Danni stared at Shiloh in glazed disbelief. 'It's ...
it's a beautiful house,' she said inadequately.

He gave her his cynical smile. 'Yes, it is quite
beautiful. But it takes more than visual beauty to
make a house a home,' he said softly, almost mockingly. 'Seeing that you're wearing your swimsuit I'll
take your change of clothes upstairs and change
myself.'

Footsteps galloped from above and Nathan in
bright red swimming trunks jumped enthusiastically
down the last few steps. 'Hi! I thought I heard you
two arrive. How's Dallas keeping your racer,
Danni?'

She smiled at his fresh young face. 'Fine,
Nathan.'

He was a nice-looking boy, in his mid-teens, and

his face held an open welcoming smile. His hair was dark and relatively closely cropped and, other than a hint of that same humour around his mouth, Danni could see little resemblance between the brothers. Nathan was as dark as Shiloh was fair.

'Hey, congratulations on becoming my prospective sister-in-law, by the way.' He gave her a noisy kiss on the cheek. 'Shiloh told me this morning, but I'd already guessed how you two felt about each other,' he grinned. 'Every time I mentioned Shiloh to you last Sunday, Danni, you went all red and flustered and when I mentioned Dallas to Shiloh he turned green. The writing was on the wall.' He laughed at them both.

'Quite the little clairvoyant, my young brother,' remarked Shiloh drily. 'How about showing Danni out to the pool while I take her things upstairs?'

'Seriously, Danni,' said Nathan, as they walked out to the pool, 'I'm really glad you're marrying Shiloh. He needs some good breaks. After the . . .' he bit his lip. 'Well, he's been through some really down times and sometimes I thought he would surely crack up under the strain. But he didn't. I think he's a great guy, Danni, the best, even if he is my brother.'

'What are you two talking about so earnestly?' asked Shiloh, striding out from the courtyard. In the bright sunlight the scars on his leg told their own story, and Danni's heart contracted painfully.

'I was just telling Danni she should reconsider about marrying you,' teased Nathan. 'I told her if she waited a couple of years she could have me,' he laughed.

'Oh, can she? We'll see about that,' said his brother, and tossed him bodily into the blue water.

The three of them spent an enjoyable afternoon in

the pool, and Nathan's company kept the atmosphere on an even keel. After they had been relaxing in the long low chairs beside the pool for an hour or so after their swim they moved inside to shower and change.

'I've put your things in my room,' said Shiloh as they walked up the stairs. 'I'll use the guest bathroom.' He opened a door and motioned Danni inside as Nathan walked further down the hall to his own room. 'The shower's through that door and I've put a clean towel on the rack for you.'

'You don't have to give up your bedroom, Shiloh. I can use the guestroom.' Danni became aware that they were virtually alone, dressed only in their brief swimwear, shut off from the rest of the house, and she turned instinctively back to the half-opened door.

But Shiloh moved quickly, reaching from behind her, shutting the door with a sharp, explosive click, leaning one hand on it to keep it closed. 'I like your bikini,' he said, a teasing smile in his voice.

Danni's pulses accelerated. She couldn't make the move to face him as she felt his eyes moving down over the rounded contours of her body, working his way with slow deliberation back to her shoulder before he moved to brush his lips across her sun-warmed softness.

Then she did turn and he put his other hand on the door, imprisoning her in the circle of his arms, and her face flushed at his nearness.

'Neither of us need resort to the guestroom,' he said softly, his lips turning to the other shoulder. 'We could conserve water and shower together.'

Danni had retreated until her hands and back were pressed against the flat of the door.

'Mmm, delicious,' he murmured, and moved his mouth up to tease her earlobe.

'Shiloh, your parents will be home any minute,' Danni began, fighting her body's responses to his caresses.

He held himself apart from her and only his lips touched her, setting her aflame. Those lips moved from her earlobe, slowly over her jaw and were drawn like a magnet to the softness of her mouth. And as their lips met his control seemed to snap and their bodies came together with mutual abandon in a feverish hunger, as it had been that morning, as though the time in between had never been.

Danni's arms moved around his naked back, sliding sensuously over the smooth muscular firmness of him, her own body arching against his as they leant together against the closed door, lost to all but the needs of their heightened senses. Her bikini top fell to the floor and his hands moved downwards, destroying all her self-control, shutting out all her thoughts of hate, of revenge. She groaned softly in pleasure and Shiloh lifted her in his arms and stalked towards the bed.

'Hey, you two!' Nathan's tap on the door halted Shiloh in mid-stride. 'Mum and Dad have just arrived, so you'd better break up your canoodling. I'll keep them busy while you get yourselves together.' And he walked down the hall chuckling.

Shiloh swore and went to continue towards the bed, but Danni struggled in his arms. He allowed her to slide to the floor and ran his fingers through his hair in exasperation.

'Very bad timing all round,' he said, his eyes moving downwards, and Danni wrapped her arms about herself in dawning horror.

If they hadn't been interrupted ...

The look in Shiloh's eyes changed from irritation to renewed arousal and she ran for the shower room. Closing the door, she heard him chuckle.

'My time will come, Danni Mathieson, and then you won't be able to run away from me. And somehow I don't think you'll much want to,' he said confidently.

Danni held her breath until she heard the outer door close behind him. Only then did she move dazedly into the shower recess, allowing the cool shower spray to fall on her burning cheeks and equally flaming body.

The whole episode had left her feeling absolutely disgusted with herself. How could she have allowed Shiloh to touch her like that? Especially now with their fiasco of a wedding to take place so soon? However, if it had left her feeling disgusted then it had at least taught her one thing. She must ensure that she kept him at arm's length at all costs, because she was not at all certain that she could trust her traitorous body where Shiloh O'Rourke was concerned.

It took some time for Danni to regain some semblance of self-possession, but she made herself go through the motions of changing into her dress, a short simply styled design in a soft pastel green material, moving slowly about Shiloh's rather austere room. She slipped her plain white high-heeled shoes on to her feet and stood in the middle of the room. Her hair was combed, her light make-up had been applied, and now she must go down to face his parents.

She felt a flutter of nervousness. They were obviously extremely well off, in a far more elite economi-

cal class than she lived in, but they were still Shiloh's
parents and they would expect certain things of the
girl he was to marry. In fact, she must convince them
that she was so taken by their elder son that she was
going to marry him in one short week's time. She
sank nervously on to the bed, glancing at her pale
face in the long mirror on his wardrobe, looking for
any courage she might find in her own reflection.

Her eyes were caught by the corner of a framed
picture standing on the floor almost concealed by
the bureau. She walked across and looked down at
it. It faced the wall and now that she looked at the
bareness of the wall above the bureau she was almost
sure it had been taken down from there. Yes, the
hook was still in the wall. She lifted the picture carefully out until she could turn it towards her.

Her hands shook until she had to lower it in case
it fell from her hands and smashed on the floor. It
was a racing shot, a black and white photograph,
and there in the background was a distinctive bill-
board that could only be Sandown. And it could
only have been taken in Shiloh's last race, in an
earlier lap, because on the curve were three cars.

The first Formula 5000, a dark one, had 'Rourkey' printed in large clear letters across the front
and the car immediately behind it, close on its tail,
was number twenty-three with 'Mathieson' written
artistically on the side of the cockpit. The third one,
partially obscured, would be Don Christie. The faces
of the drivers were not distinguishable behind the
racing helmets, but Danni knew just how they both
looked, knew both of their faces would be tense with
concentration, their breathing regular, their eyes
sharpened to watch for each minute movement.
Shiloh must have just passed the other two, and

would have had two more cars in front of him.

Why had he taken the photograph down? Did he think it would upset her? Or did it remind him of his own guilt? Maybe that was the reason he had it hanging in his room, so that he would constantly remember his tragic mistake. Danni burned in anticipation of watching his face when she took her revenge.

'Danni?' Nathan tapped lightly on the door. 'You ready yet?'

She moved quickly, sliding the photo back into its place behind the bureau and, pulling herself together, she put a smile on her face and walked across to the door. 'Sure, Nathan, I'm ready.'

He smiled easily. 'Aw, don't worry, Danni. They'll love you.'

If only it was that simple, Danni thought, as they walked down the steps.

There were three people in the living-room below. Shiloh was to one side, apart from his parents, giving the glass he held his undivided attention. He looked smoothly attractive in a conservative pair of grey flared tailored slacks and a white knit shirt, the collar of which was open at the neck showing the firm column of his throat and the beginning of a mat of curling fair hair on his broad chest.

Conan O'Rourke stood across the room and he was frowning at his son. He was a tall broad-shouldered man, his dark lounge suit sitting well on his solidly built frame. His dark hair was almost completely grey and he looked exactly what he was, a distinguished and successful businessman. That he was Shiloh's father there was no doubt. He held himself in the same firm upright manner and there was some resemblance in his features.

His frowning countenance and Shiloh's set expression pointed to there having been a disagreement over something, but whether or not it concerned herself Danni couldn't tell, as nothing was said as she approached the stairs with Nathan.

'Ah, this can only be Danielle,' the woman sitting on the lounge chair by Conan O'Rourke said pleasantly, setting her glass of sherry on the coffee table as she stood up and walked across towards Danni. 'We've heard so much about you from both of our sons. I'm Estie O'Rourke.' She took Danni's hands and kissed her lightly on the cheek. Although her smile was pleasant her eyes were looking sharply at the younger girl, weighing her up. 'We're pleased to meet you at last.'

'How do you do, Mrs O'Rourke.' Danni had to admit to being a little overawed by this glamorous woman. She was a good four inches taller than Danni and looked far too young to be Shiloh's mother.

'Please call me Estie,' she laughed gaily. 'Everyone does.' She had just a slight American accent and for a woman who must be all of fifty years old at the very least Estie O'Rourke carried her age exceptionally well. She was tall and slim with a good figure and her dark hair was coiled neatly in a chignon. Her make-up was flawless and there was something about her eyes that reminded Danni of Shiloh. In the lapel of her dark tailored suit she wore a diamond pin and two large diamonds flashed on the fingers of her left hand.

'Here's your sherry, Estie.' Shiloh had moved over to the bar. 'What will you have, Danni? Ouzo and lemonade, wasn't it?'

'Oh, no. No, thank you, Shiloh. I'll have a sherry, too,' Danni said hurriedly, imagining what would happen if she drank ouzo on an empty stomach. And her stomach did feel empty. She had been far too over-stimulated to eat much lunch and somehow she didn't think she'd make a very good impression on the O'Rourkes if she sat in a corner and went to sleep.

Shiloh's father had moved across the deep pile carpet and it was Estie who introduced her husband to Danni.

'So this is Danni,' he said evenly.

'Another beer, Conan?' asked Shiloh, and took the empty glass from his father, his eyes watching his father's face. Like a cat ready to pounce, thought Danni, watching the clash of some discordance between them.

'I suppose it's Coke for me,' sighed Nathan. 'Sure it won't be too strong for me?' he asked, not abashed by the frown his father turned on him.

'Shiloh tells us you work in a library, Danni,' Estie put in smoothly, sipping her sherry.

'Yes, at Burleigh Heads,' replied Danni, 'and I enjoy it very much.'

'It's a career I would have chosen myself,' said Shiloh's mother. 'I'm an inveterate reader. In fact, I'm reading a very enjoyable novel at the moment.'

Danni felt herself relaxing as she began to discuss favourite books and authors with Estie O'Rourke. Shiloh and Conan added little to the conversation, but Estie's relaxed and friendly manner put Danni at her ease. By the time their housekeeper announced that dinner was ready Danni felt almost herself.

The meal was delicious and the conversation flowed quite normally, although Danni sensed an underlying reserve in Conan O'Rourke. But she told herself it was most probably his nature, for his wife seemed quite calm and amicable.

They had reached the dessert stage when Estie smiled across at Danni. 'It's nice to have a face now to put to your name. When the boys spoke of you I was extremely curious to meet you.'

'Oh, dear, I hope everything they told you was good,' Danni laughed a little selfconsciously.

'Yes, it was,' she smiled. 'Although I was a trifle confused as I couldn't correlate their conflicting descriptions. On the one hand you were a very nice-looking librarian and on the other a competent and successful motor racing driver.'

Shiloh's father wiped his mouth on his napkin. 'Motor racing seems to be a strange occupation for a young lady,' he said.

'Yes, but I enjoy doing it,' Danni felt the tension in the room. The air was so thick she could have cut it with a knife. Even Estie O'Rourke's mouth seemed to be held stiffly as though she waited a little uneasily for her husband's next statement.

Before he could comment Nathan beamed across at Danni. 'Wow! Danni's really something out there on the track. I don't know how she has the nerve to do it. My heart was in my mouth most of the time just watching the race.'

'I think I must have a screw loose somewhere, Nathan, don't you?' She laughed and fell silent when she saw the look of disapproval on Conan O'Rourke's face.

'Shiloh tells us that you two would like to get married,' said Conan, turning his frown on his younger son before looking back at Danni.

Danni glanced at Shiloh and he spoke before she could formulate a reply. 'We've decided on next Saturday. We'll have a celebrant perform the ceremony out at Danni's father's property up in the valley. It's a pleasant rural setting and there'll only be our immediate families present,' he said firmly.

'Don't you think you're rushing into this?' Conan looked straight at Danni. 'You scarcely know each other.'

Danni flushed under his steady gaze. 'We'd like it to be next weekend. It ... it seems to fit in with Shiloh's business and the racing calendar.'

'Oh, yes, the racing.' His lips curled derogatorily. 'When my son told me he was getting married I thought, in fact, I hoped, he'd finished with these lunatic plans of his, but I can see I was wrong, more's the pity.'

'Conan.' Shiloh's voice was cold and controlled. 'We decided not to discuss all that tonight.'

'*You* decided we'd not discuss it,' exclaimed his father. 'I can't understand why you would possibly want to continue with that senseless sport when it all but killed you last year. If I'd had to live with that day on my conscience like you have had to I'd never want to see another race track, let alone begin racing again!'

Danni's face paled. It was as though the final item of proof of her suspicions had been laid before her. If Shiloh's own father believed him responsible for that crash then surely he must be guilty. And why should Shiloh want to continue racing anyway? If Chris Damien took him on he was a fool.

Through her lashes she watched Shiloh's face for his reactions, but if she expected to see any sign of guilt in his face she was sadly disappointed. The only outward sign he gave that he was disturbed was a certain paleness about his mouth.

Conan O'Rourke turned to Danni. 'Surely you

don't want your husband taking a car out on to the track, a car that he's determined to have kill him before he's much older? That's if he doesn't kill someone else in the process,' he added bitterly, his face flushed with anger.

'Racing is something I like to do,' Shiloh said flatly, his jaw set.

'Oh! It was something young Christie and Rick Mathieson liked to do too, and what consolation was that for their families? Does it mean anything to them?' Conan's eyes flashed to Danni and his face paled. 'Mathieson?' he repeated softly.

'Rick was Danni's brother.' Shiloh's voice held no expression and Nathan looked down at his plate with embarrassment.

Danni was incapable of uttering a sound and she looked across at Shiloh, her face white, seeing Rick there between them again.

'Conan! Shiloh! Please!' Estie's beringed fingers moved agitatedly at her throat. 'What will we gain from raking over painful memories? You've upset Danni and she's our guest and our future daughter-in-law. I think we should allow them to sort it out for themselves. All of this is getting us nowhere.'

Conan's eyes moved from his son's face to Danni and he sighed again. 'My apologies, Danni. I was unaware ...' he coughed. 'I didn't intend to make any mention of all this, but, as you can imagine, I feel most strongly about it. I feel it's time Shiloh came into our engineering business.'

'Of ... of course,' Danni murmured. 'I can understand your feelings, Mr O'Rourke.'

Shiloh's mother relaxed visibly and hurriedly led the conversation back to less volatile topics, although the brief altercation at the dinner table lay over them for the duration of the evening.

By ten o'clock Danni was trying valiantly to stifle her yawns. The entirely unreal day had taken its toll and she felt emotionally drained, desiring only to climb into bed and have the blessed relief of a dreamless sleep.

'Want to go home?' Shiloh asked her softly.

'I am a little tired,' she said, 'if your parents would excuse me.'

'Of course, my dear,' said Estie, standing up, trying not to appear relieved. 'We've enjoyed meeting you, haven't we, Conan?'

Her husband added his assurance to this and Danni tried not to give a thankful sigh as she walked out into the courtyard behind Shiloh.

Nathan made to follow them along the wide pathway to the garage.

'And where do you think you're going, Nathan?' asked Shiloh.

'I thought I'd come along for the ride. Why?' he asked innocently.

'I don't remember asking you,' remarked Shiloh.

'Oh, let him come, Shiloh,' said Danni quickly. To be alone with Shiloh again tonight was more than she could contend with.

Shiloh frowned and then shrugged his shoulders. 'Seems I'm outvoted.' He turned to his brother. 'All right, if you want to be cramped up in the back seat of the Lotus.'

Neither Danni nor Shiloh added much to the conversation on the short drive to Danni's house except to answer Nathan's questions where necessary. In fact, Nathan did enough talking for the three of them.

Shiloh walked around the front of the car and

held the door open for Danni. She was barely on the footpath when Nathan had climbed out of the back of the car and stood beside them.

'Would you mind waiting in the car while I see Danni to the door?' Shiloh gave his brother a push.

Nathan went to protest, looked from one to the other, nodded knowingly and grinning, subsided into the seat Danni had vacated. 'Okay. 'Night, Danni. See you at the wedding.'

'Yes. Goodnight, Nathan,' she said, and moved quickly up the pathway to the house, conscious of Shiloh's long strides right behind her. At the top of the steps his hand covered hers as she went to insert the key in the lock.

His lips moved to find hers in the darkness and she turned her head so that his kiss fell on her cheek. Then his hands were on either side of her face and his lips captured hers almost in desperation. 'How am I going to last out this week?' he murmured. 'Mmm, I've been wanting to continue our little interlude in my room all evening.' He kissed her again as Danni's hands went around his waist of their own volition. 'I could go on like this all night. However, I can imagine my nosey young brother putting a time limit on our goodnight.' His lips moved over her eyes to her earlobes down over the softness of her neck and when she moaned responsively his arms crushed her to him, his lips returning to her lips, his kiss searing her mouth, drawing forth a response which frightened her with its intensity.

He tore himself away from her and leant back against the railings of the steps. 'Roll on Saturday,' he laughed huskily.

'I'd better go inside.' Danni was still trembling from his kiss. 'Goodnight, Shiloh.'

'Danni, about my father ...' he stopped and swore softly under his breath. 'No matter,' he said quietly. 'What are your plans for tomorrow?' His hand on her arm detained her, his thumb moving gently over her smooth skin.

'I thought I'd go out to Mallaroo. I'd like to spend some time with Pop,' she said quickly, hoping he wouldn't want to accompany her.

There was a slight pause. 'All right.' His hand slid down her arm and he raised her hand to his lips. 'By the way, do you need this ring for a few days?' He touched the simple dress ring she wore on her right hand.

'No. Why?'

'I'll use it to gauge the size for your rings. I'll pick them up in Sydney next week if you don't mind leaving the choice to me.'

Danni nodded. 'You're going to Sydney again?'

'Yes.' There was a strange note in his voice, almost as though he didn't want to go. 'I'll be back by Saturday, though. Wild horses won't keep me away!' He kissed her lightly on the cheek.

Danni slept deeply and soundly that night and rose early to drive out to Mallaroo. All morning she kept her mind away from any thought of the wedding. She wouldn't allow herself to think about it. She went about the farm with her father and although he also made no mention of Shiloh or the wedding it lay between them, causing a tension that tugged at Danni's heart.

It wasn't until she was sitting alone on the patio after lunch that she saw Dallas Byrne's red head moving towards the house. Her father had not yet returned from the workshop where he was overseeing the reshoeing of one of the horses.

Danni's heart sank. She could tell by the stiffness of Dallas's body as he strode purposefully towards her that he had heard about her wedding and she wished fervently that she didn't have to face him. The very last thing she wanted to do at the moment was to discuss it all with Dallas.

'Danni, what's going on? Your father tells me you're getting married next weekend,' Dallas's face was tense with anger, 'to that ... that damned O'Rourke fellow. Is it true?'

'Yes, Dallas, it's true. Shiloh and I have decided to get married,' Danni told him quietly.

'Have you gone stark raving mad, girl?' He stood aggressively in front of her. 'If you believed only half of the reports about the crash you'd have to agree that he killed your brother,' he said brutally.

Danni put her hands over her ears. 'I don't care what half the reports said. We're getting married next weekend, and surely it's no business of anyone but Shiloh and myself.'

'It's criminal that he should be walking around free. If it was anyone else they'd be in jail,' retorted Dallas.

'I don't want to discuss it, Dallas. No matter what you say, it won't change a thing.'

Dallas stood impotently in front of her, his face red with anger and hurt, and Danni had to drop her eyes.

'No good is going to come of this marriage, Danni.' Dallas's hands gripped her shoulders painfully. 'Rick's death—it will always be there between you. Can't you see that?'

'Dallas, please! You're hurting me.' Danni pulled away from him.

'What the hell do you think you're doing to me?'

He strode across to the edge of the patio and stood with his back to her, hands on hips.

'Look, Dallas, I didn't set out to deliberately cause you any distress—I like you too much for that. We've been good friends and I'd like us to stay that way. I told you right from the start . . .' Danni's voice faded away.

Dallas sighed. 'I know. It's my own stupid fault.' He turned and walked back to stand in front of her. 'But I do feel there's something not right about this marriage. Even I can tell that you're no more in love with O'Rourke than I am,' his lip curled, 'so why the almighty haste? Has he got some hold over you?' A thought crossed his mind and his face turned a shade redder. 'My God, you're not—well, pregnant, are you?'

'Of course I'm not. And I resent that, Dallas,' Danni said angrily, and he had the grace to look a little ashamed of himself and they fell silent for a few moments.

'I'm sorry, Danni, I shouldn't have . . . Do you still want me to head off with the car tomorrow week as planned, or are you going to give up racing?' he asked.

'Of course. It doesn't change anything. I'll be racing at Oran Park in two weeks as planned and I'd like you to stay with me. I can't do it without you,' Danni appealed to him. 'I mean that, Dallas.'

'Okay.' He walked towards the steps. 'I have to get back to work.' He turned when he reached the bottom. 'And none of this changes how I feel about you, Danni. If you need me for anything, any time, I'll be there.' He smiled crookedly. 'And that includes picking up the pieces afterwards!'

Picking up the pieces afterwards. The words

echoed in Danni's mind as she stood on the patio gazing out over the green lawns, absently running her hand over the smooth railings. Picking up the pieces. Somehow she couldn't see Shiloh breaking, and in the cold light of day she had grave doubts that she would come out the victor in any confrontation she had with him.

CHAPTER EIGHT

DANNI stood in her bedroom at Mallaroo. She wore a long pale blue dress that left her shoulders bare, the bodice moulding her firm young breasts and the skirt falling to the floor in soft drifting folds. Her dark hair fell in liquid waves about her lightly tanned shoulders. She wore no veil, yet in three-quarters of an hour she would be married. In her adolescent dreams she had always seen herself in a church, in traditional white, the organ playing, an aura of happiness radiating from everyone, her father proud and straight beside her, her brother ... She closed her mind and blinked a mist from before her eyes.

Today there was no happiness inside her. Any sensation she experienced when she allowed herself to think was one of numb acceptance of the way things had to be. If a part of her wished that her girlhood dreams were being fulfilled she hastily buried those thoughts beneath a cold determination. For today she would have her revenge on Shiloh O'Rourke.

She shivered and the small sliver of doubt found a tiny chink in the tight web of control she had fixed about herself, and that sliver of doubt began to grow within her. Memories of the touch of Shiloh's mouth on hers came back to haunt her and her hand moved tremblingly to touch her parted lips, while Dallas's words spun about her mind. Picking up the pieces.

Pulling herself stiffly together, she mustered all her self-possession. More thoughts along those lines and she would fall completely apart.

No. At all times she must remember Rick, remember that had it not been for Shiloh O'Rourke Rick would have been here today. None of this would be happening if Rick was here today, taunted an inner voice, and she experienced an hysterical desire to laugh and laugh and never stop. In fact, she could feel the sound rising in her throat when there was a tap on her door and Lisa walked in.

'Oh, Danni, you look divine! I'm so happy for you.' Lisa's eyes were bright with tears. 'I knew it— I just knew it the moment I saw him that he was the one for you. It's so romantic!' She clasped her hands together and Danni tried to put some warmth into her smile.

'They've arrived—Shiloh and his family, that is,' Lisa informed her. 'And Dallas brought the celebrant about a quarter of an hour ago. Talking about Dallas, he seems to be taking it all in his stride. Wasn't he upset when he found out about you and Shiloh?'

Danni nodded. 'I felt awful about it, but—well, I never led Dallas to believe things could ever be serious between us.'

'No, I know you didn't. And I suppose I couldn't see Dallas taking it any way other than calmly.' Lisa grinned impishly at Danni. 'Now Shiloh would have been different. He'd have slung you over his shoulder and carted you off, and that's the truth.'

Danni tried hard to laugh with the other girl.

'Shiloh looks gorgeous, too. Wait till you see him. Mmm! You two make such a lovely couple.' Lisa beamed, starry-eyed.

'You look very attractive yourself, Lisa,' said Danni, and the thought crossed Danni's mind that Lisa, her face glowing with excitement, looked more like a bride than she did.

'So Shiloh's brother just told me.' She raised her eyes. 'He's cute, too. Pity he wasn't a couple of years older.' Lisa glanced at the clock on Danni's dressing table. 'It's nearly time. Your father said he'd be coming up in a minute.' She handed Danni her bouquet of rich white frangipani and then lifted her matching bridesmaid's bouquet of apricot frangipani. 'Come on out into the living-room and we can peep out at the setting under the trees. It's really lovely. Everyone's here already.'

Danni looked around her bedroom again, in something of a farewell, as Lisa opened the door. In a way it was a farewell, because one way or another things would never be quite the same again. Her eyes rose to the photo of her brother and she took a deep resolute breath.

Her father had generously suggested that they live in the house at Broadbeach after they were married, until they decided where they wanted to set up house. Set up house. She shivered and gave herself a mental shake. Things weren't going to change, she told herself firmly. She would keep them the same. She would still have this room, and she would still live in the house at Broadbeach during the week while she went to work. What Shiloh did she didn't care. Somehow she couldn't see him staying around after she'd finished with him tonight. This was for Rick. She had to hold on to that thought.

'Danni?' Lisa was waiting at the door. 'You're just not with it, are you?' she smiled indulgently. 'Come on, girl! Stop mooning about Shiloh or you'll be late for your wedding.'

Jock Mathieson, looking a little out of character in his brand new suit, walked on to the patio as the two girls entered the living-room. 'Ready, love?' he asked, and Danni nodded.

'Come on, then.' He tried to laugh. 'I'm as nervous as a kitten, but don't tell anyone I admitted it!' His eyes didn't quite meet hers and she felt her heart ache painfully.

Oh, Pop, bear with me for a little while, Danni silently begged him. A few days and it will be over and we can get back to going on as we were before Shiloh O'Rourke came on to the scene with such devastating results. And she closed herself off from the little voice that jeered her, told her that the way things were would never be again.

The short walk across the drive to join the group of about twenty people on the lawn under the shady native gums was the longest walk of Danni's life. Then before she knew it, she was standing beside Shiloh and she could feel his eyes on her. She couldn't resist one quick glance in his direction and in that one swift glance her breath caught painfully in her chest.

He wore a cream dress shirt with his dark brown tailored suit which fitted his tall body to perfection, hugging his broad muscular shoulders, tapering to his narrow waist and moulding his long legs, the darkness of the colour emphasising the fairness of his hair. For one split second his tawny eyes smiled into hers and she almost cried out as a shaft of pure and mutual unity flashed between them.

'Dearly beloved ...' began the celebrant, and those two words reverberated about inside Danni's mind. Dearly beloved. Dearly beloved. Beloved. She had to fight that same almost hysterical urge to laugh and suddenly realised unshed tears were burning her eyes. There was an unreality about it all, as though it wasn't, it couldn't be happening.

She hardly took it in and yet, quite vividly, she remembered Nathan winking at her as he passed Shiloh their rings, and she was numbly aware that Shiloh kissed her gently on the lips and that her father seemed to have to resort to blowing his nose after the ceremony.

Hired caterers served the wedding guests in the large dining room at Mallaroo and Danni managed to eat a little, to drink some wine, to be merry. Once she noticed Shiloh and her father standing together talking, neither of them smiling. Speeches were made and there was much laughter and the usual good-natured teasing of the bride and groom. Just like any other wedding, Danni thought coldly.

'Danni.' Shiloh's mother touched her on the arm and she turned, blinking, trying to pull her thoughts together. 'You look beautiful, my dear.' Estie kissed her cheek. 'And Shiloh's so proud of you.'

'Thank you,' Danni murmured, and they both turned to glance across at Shiloh as he stood talking to Bill Peterson. Danni's mind was completely numb, refused to function. She watched Shiloh, but any thoughts she might have had refused to form in her mind, didn't compute.

'He deserves someone like you, Danni,' Estie was saying, and a wave of feeling caused Danni's heart to behave erratically as Shiloh moved his head and the light caught an unruly lock of fair hair as it sprang out of place.

'You both have the same interests,' continued Estie, 'so perhaps you can understand this craving he's always had for speed. I can't pretend I like him racing, I never have, but he's been through hell these past months, irrespective of his physical injuries. As you know, the doctors really didn't expect him to walk again.' There were tears in Estie's eyes. 'He suffered so much. Especially with all those rumours after ...'

Danni felt her own eyes fill with tears and Estie patted her hand. 'I'm sorry if I've upset you, but I felt I had to say it, Danni. He's my son and I love him, and he needs you very much.'

Danni's heart was fluttering again. Of course his mother was prejudiced. But that same niggling of doubt found that same chink in her armour. She was so confused.

But according to Dallas everyone had cast aside the findings of the Board of Enquiry, and to a man seemed to hold Shiloh responsible. Surely they wouldn't all think that way without there being some grounds for the innuendoes? Where there was smoke there had to be fire.

Her brother was dead, at the high point of his career, for had he finished that race in even fifth placing Rick would have taken out the highest aggregate of points to make him Champion of the Year. The futility of it all washed over her once again in waves of frustration.

Her gaze moved back to Shiloh and in that moment he turned, in the act of lifting a glass to his lips, and their eyes met. The emotion that raced through Danni like wildfire was not hate or revenge and she was unaware of the softening of her features.

Shiloh smiled slightly and excused himself from Bill before beginning to walk across to her. Estie squeezed her arm again.

'Here's Shiloh coming. I'll leave you two together,' she said quietly. 'I'm happy for you both. Maybe now all these vicious rumours about Shiloh will come to an end.'

Rumours. Did Estie mean ...? What did she mean? A horrible thought took hold of her, wrapped itself around her heart and squeezed excruciatingly. Was that the reason he had been so adamant about marrying her? To kill all the rumours about his involvement in the crash? No one would believe he was guilty when Rick Mathieson's own sister had ...

'Do you suppose they'd think we were rude if we left now?' he whispered in her ear, a smile teasing the corners of his mouth. He looked relaxed and some of the strain seemed to have smoothed from his face. But Danni had to physically check herself from flinching from his touch as his hand rested lightly on her waist.

'It's early yet.' She felt panic rise inside her. She wasn't ready to be alone with him, to face what she had set out to do.

'Well, I could always begin to kiss you passionately right here in front of everyone.' His lips touched the edge of her jaw.

'You wouldn't!' Her eyes flew to his face.

'I would.'

Yes, he would. Although his lips smiled, the creases in his cheeks deepening, his eyes flashed steel. 'I'll go and tell Pop.' Danni's face flushed beneath the force in those eyes and her hands were clasped together until the knuckles showed white.

Half an hour later they were driving down the narrow winding road to the coast.

'Tired?' he asked as his hands moved expertly on the steering wheeel.

'A little.' Danni's voice wasn't quite her own.

'Why not recline the seat and have a doze? I'll wake you when we get to the hotel,' he was saying indulgently.

'Yes, I might do that.' Anything, so that she wouldn't have to make conversation, so that her eyes wouldn't have to turn to the firmness of his profile.

Her head was full of dozens of impressions. The look in her father's eyes as he kissed her goodbye. The feeling that, no matter what, she had let him down. And Shiloh's mother and those few words that had chilled Danni's partially thawed heart. She smiled cynically to herself. Maybe both of them, Shiloh and herself, would get what they wanted from this fiasco of a marriage.

Surprisingly she did sleep, and his hand gently moving on her arm dragged her from her slumber to blink in the dimness of the under road level car park of the high-rise hotel on the waterfront in Surfers Paradise.

'Wake up, sleepyhead, we're here,' he said caressingly, and walked around to hold her door open for her.

Danni walked slowly across to the large plate glass window and stared sightlessly down at the fairyland of lights far below that ran along the coast, the moonlight highlighting the restless motion of the sea. Shivering slightly, she wrapped her arms about her trembling body. As she turned slightly she caught the reflection of Shiloh's movements in the shiny surface of the glass.

He had removed his suit coat and bow tie and now he was unbuttoning the cuffs of his shirt, his eyes looking in her direction causing her to shiver even more. Once again she was reminded of a jungle cat prowling, stalking, for ever on his guard.

A tap on the door of their suite brought her heart into her mouth and she spun around as Shiloh opened the door and spoke to the uniformed waiter who wheeled a small trolley into the room. On the trolley sat an ice bucket containing a bottle of champagne and two fine-stemmed glasses.

Shiloh closed the door after the man. 'Just what the doctor ordered, or in this case, just what I ordered,' he said with a smile. He filled the two glasses with the bubbly liquid, replacing the bottle in the ice bucket, and holding a glass out to Danni.

Feeling like an automaton, Danni moved across and took the glass in numbed fingers.

Shiloh lifted his own glass and raised it in her direction. 'To us,' he said softly.

Danni blinked at him as though he was a stranger she hadn't seen before and the glass trembled in her hand.

Watching her closely Shiloh stopped his glass before it reached his mouth and he leant over and removed the glass from her hand and set both glasses on the trolley. His hands took hold of her shoulders and turned her to face him. 'What's the trouble, Danni? You've been looking at me as if I was someone you'd just met on the street.'

'Don't be silly.' Her face almost cracked with her smile. 'Nothing's the matter. What could be the matter? I'm just tired, that's all.'

He looked at her warily for a moment. 'I'm ready for bed myself, but I'm not saying that tiredness is driving me there,' he said huskily, drawing her against him, bending his head to run his lips along her jawline. 'Who needs champagne anyway?' His white teeth teased her earlobe.

At the nearness of his body a sensual euphoria began to wrap Danni within its tentacles and she knew if she was to make her move it had to be now while she still had some semblance of control over her actions. She had to hold on to Rick's memory, her father's pain and now Shiloh's mother's revelations. She tensed and pushed her hands against his chest, taking him by surprise and breaking the lightly confident hold he had on her. His expression was more puzzled than anything else, and a surge of guilt rose within her. Her only defence against it was her anger, and it rose in combat.

'Don't touch me! I can't bear for you to touch me!' she said angrily, while part of her cried out to stop this now, not wanting to watch the change come over the planes of his strong face. Remember! she screamed at herself.

The puzzlement died and in its place appeared an anger to match and surpass her own. 'For heaven's sake, Danni, something has to be the matter. I don't remember you fending me off before. In fact, I'd say you gave me the green light right from the start. So what's the beef?' He ran a hand through his hair. 'Don't try to tell me that if Nathan hadn't interrupted us last weekend there wouldn't be any need for this outraged virgin act. Or is that your thing, Danni? Lead them on and leave them hanging?'

'No, it's not my thing.' High spots of colour burned in her cheeks. 'But you're partially right about the act. It was an act. I pretended I enjoyed your lovemaking just so I could bring you to this moment. And it was remarkably easy.' Danni cringed inside herself. It was as though she was standing apart from her body, watching the whole sordid scene unfold.

Shiloh watched her with eyes narrowed. 'I suppose there has to be a reason for all this,' he said flatly, expressionlessly.

'You don't think I could genuinely be in love with the man who killed my brother, do you? Rick and I were close, and his death shouldn't go unavenged,' she replied just as coolly. 'And then there's my father—Rick's death has broken him. And you're responsible.'

His face was carved granite, white about the mouth, and his eyes raked her angrily, a cold, steely anger that sparked a quiver of fear within her. 'What the hell do you mean by that?' he barked out, one hand imprisoning her wrist in a vice-like grip. 'I told you I had nothing to do with the accident. I thought we'd been through all that before, Danni, and I'm damned if I'm going to keep on saying it for the rest of my life. Not to you. Not to anyone.'

'If you weren't responsible for the pile-up then why did all the racing journalists say that you were?' she demanded, trying futilely to drag her arm from his biting hold.

'They didn't say I was to blame,' he said bitterly, 'because if they had I would have sued them for libel. Unfortunately I have no say over what people read into newspaper reports.'

'What about everyone in the racing fraternity, they all seem to agree with the reports?'

'Rubbish! They all know the risks involved in motor racing and they would no more come out and accuse me of causing that accident than fly. Look, Danni, all of the blokes in that race, in every motor race, know the chances they're taking. It's part of it all. Rick knew, just as young Don Christie knew.' He ran a hand through his hair. 'Who's supposed to have convinced you of all this, anyway? Or maybe I can make a guess. Dallas Byrne.'

'Well, Dallas said ...'

'So Dallas said ... And that's enough said, isn't it? He's so green with jealousy he'd say anything to get to you, and you know it.' Shiloh thrust her hand away. 'God, I'm sick of all this! It's followed me around until I can taste it in my mouth and I've had it up to my back teeth.' He looked at her steadily. 'I'll say it once more and I'll never say it again, and you can take it or leave it. I was in no way responsible for your brother's death. It was an unfortunate accident, no more. It wasn't a reflection on Rick's driving. He simply didn't have time to swerve to avoid that collision. Okay? Finished! Now for heaven's sake, let the whole thing rest and let's go to bed.' He picked up a glass of champagne and downed it in one gulp, giving the empty glass a wry look before he set it carelessly back on the trolley.

'Yes, I will go to bed. But not with you. I ... I still hold you responsible for Rick's death and—well, we can stay married until I decide I don't want to be married any longer.'

'You can't be serious! No one would be crazy enough to ...' He stepped towards her, his fingers biting into her arms. 'And what's to stop me forcing you to perform your wifely duties?' he asked harshly, 'because I've a feeling it wouldn't take much to change your scheming twisted little mind?'

A flicker of fear flew to Danni's eyes and her pale face flushed red at the implications in his words.

For a moment she thought he meant what he said, but his lips twisted and he flung her from him.

'Don't worry, you're safe from me. I've never had to force myself on any woman and I'm not about to start with you.' He walked across and picking up his coat moved towards the door. As he passed the drinks trolley he paused for a moment and, lifting the opened bottle of champagne, carried it with him, and as he opened the door he glanced back at Danni, his face set and cold.

'Where are you going?' she couldn't stop herself asking.

'Don't tell me you care, Mrs O'Rourke?' he said scathingly. 'I'm going for a long walk. If I stay here I might change my mind about you, and we can't have that, now can we? Besides, cold showers have never worked with me.' He left, slamming the door after him.

For immeasurable minutes Danni stood where he had left her, the sound of the slammed door vibrating in her ears. The cold calmness within her brought welcome numbness, although a small part of her registered almost terror at the horror of what she had done. She moved quietly to the bedroom, undressing, showering, climbing into bed without allowing her mind to dwell on the fact that the bed was huge and empty, and should have been full of them both.

The whole day had been unreal, as though the entire cast were strangers and the plot a figment of some imagination. She tried to will herself to sleep, but her mind kept tossing over the day's events.

She had succeeded in her plan of revenge and she should be rejoicing, but by no stretch of the imagination could that revenge be called sweet. In fact, were she honest with herself then she would admit that the whole thing left her feeling cheap and nasty. And cold.

It was acceptable for her to call the shots, but to

learn that Shiloh also had a motive for marrying her cut her to the quick. And if she admitted it to herself it cut deeply.

But he was the one who deserved to suffer, wasn't he? she asked herself. Yes. He had taken a life, not just any life, but her own brother's life, and if she lived to be a hundred she would make him pay. And then to use her to cover it up, gloss it over. Oh, he deserved to pay! An eye for an eye. She had judged and . . . But in the eyes of the law he was not guilty.

What if he was as innocent as he professed himself to be? The tiny niggling of doubt forced itself into her mind and she immediately discarded these sympathetic thoughts before they could take hold. As it was, she knew a tiny part inside of her had been harbouring an almost fanatical desire for his innocence, and she cast this aside and concentrated on Rick, reviving her desire to avenge his death.

Rick's handsome dark face swam before her, but she found it hard to hold it there, for her brother's image kept fading, was replaced by Shiloh's face as he had left her, hard, cold and unforgiving.

She slept long after the tears dried on her cheeks and awoke slowly next morning, part of her reluctant to relinquish the forgetfulness of unconsciousness, and for a fleeting moment she was hard pressed to recognise her surroundings. But all too suddenly it all flooded back to her and the sound of the shower running in the bathroom off the bedroom had her eyes flying to the opened door.

Almost mesmerised, her eyes watched that door as she became aware that the shower had stopped running and that sounds of movement came from within. Shiloh appeared a moment later, a deep blue towel wrapped sarong-wise around his waist, droplets of moisture still clinging to his dampened hair. His face was set and his cold eyes turned from her after one contemptuous glance which took in the nervousness of her fingers as they clutched the bedclothes up to her chin in an unconscious defence. Irrelevantly she noticed he had cut his cheek shaving and her senses screamed in the silence for him to say something. Anything.

He walked across to his suitcase which had been flung open and took out fresh clothes. Her startled eyes flew open and then looked blushingly away as without a backward glance he nonchalantly removed the towel and began climbing into his shorts.

'Breakfast arrived five minutes ago,' he said as he moved into the adjoining room.

Danni scrambled out of bed and grabbing some underclothes and a pair of shorts and matching top, she ran to the bathroom, making sure she secured the door after her. When she joined him Shiloh was drinking a cup of coffee and reading the newspaper, and barely registered her presence.

Nervously she poured herself some coffee and began to eat a warm roll, although the food had a tendency to stick in her throat.

The fair head and glacial brown eyes appeared over the top of the newspaper and she almost started when he eventually spoke.

'I suppose you haven't had a change of heart after your night's rest?' he asked tersely, his eyes boring into hers.

'No.' Danni gulped a mouthful of bacon. 'No, I haven't,' she said, her voice a little stronger.

He appeared to be about to pass a comment, but his lips set in a grim line. 'So be it. Pack your things after you've eaten and I'll drop you back at Broadbeach on my way to the airport.'

'The airport? Where are you going? We're—well, we were going to stay until Tuesday.'

His eyes raked her. 'I somehow think that's point- less, don't you? Besides, there are things I can be doing down south. I had planned on leaving them until later in the week, but ...' He shrugged his shoulders. 'Of course, we can stay here if you'd like to insist,' he said coldly, 'but I warn you, Danni, if we stay I'm not going without a bed again tonight. I'll be right in there beside you. So please yourself.'

'I'll go and pack now,' she said after a pause, and silently left the room.

What remained of Danni's honeymoon she spent alone at her father's house in Broadbeach. Shiloh didn't bother to come past the front foyer. He simply deposited her suitcase, gave her a long cold look, returned to his car and drove away.

After mooching around the suddenly super-empty house she decided to use her few days off work giv- ing the whole house a thorough spring-cleaning. What was done was done, and at least the vigorous effort she put into scrubbing and polishing took her mind away from Shiloh O'Rourke. The strenuous activity had her falling exhausted into bed that first night, and it wasn't until the next day that every- thing caught up with her.

It was such a silly thing that started it all off. She was dusting the ornaments on the sideboard when her elbow caught a little china figurine of a shepherd boy. The figurine had been a childhood gift, the giver long forgotten and the occasion equally shrouded in the past, but the sight of the little shep- herd, now headless, had the tears coursing down Danni's face. She sank down on the floor with the figurine in one hand, her duster in the other, and wept without stopping. The little figurine was forgotten long before her tear-filled eyes blurred it into oblivion. She knew she really wept for herself and for Shiloh, for what might have been.

Her thoughts kept returning to those days before she had found out who he really was, and the tragic part he had played in their lives. Vividly she was back out at the practice track at Mallaroo and Shiloh was making his first breathtaking appearance in her life, the way he had mistaken her for a young boy, how he had high-handedly interfered with her car and her anger and the uncertainty at the feelings he had awoken within her at that first meeting.

Then there was the night they had gone out to dinner, the pleasure of finding each other, the dawning sensation of their mutual awareness, the almost instantaneous, physical response that had flared between them and the almost wondrous, ecstatic feeling that love could really be like that. Love? Had she been falling in love with him then? Danni sniffed self-pityingly and more tears fell unrestrained. Oh, why couldn't he have been innocent of the charges laid against him?

Maybe he is innocent, repeated a tiny voice inside her, and she clutched avidly at the thought. The Board of Enquiry would have thoroughly investigated the whole incident, and they had brought down a verdict of Not Guilty. Could Shiloh have been telling the truth? But no. The racing fraternity were a close-knit group and would protect one of their own to the end, especially if there was any doubt about his being responsible for a fatal accident.

This thought brought in its wake a terrible premonition that left her shaken and ashamed. Could she have misjudged him? Should she have simply trusted her own first impressions? His strong lean face swam before her eyes and her heartbeat accelerated. Little incidents came back to her, the way his mouth turned up at the corners, the burning desire in his cat's eyes, the safeness of his arms wound about her.

Then why were some people so set against Shiloh's innocence? Her own father even. And Dallas had said . . . She stopped. She did only have Dallas's word that the majority of people involved in the racing game held Shiloh responsible. But her father believed it, didn't he?

She turned over what had been said that night. Dallas had done most of the talking really and her father had sat shocked, stunned. But he hadn't said a word in Shiloh's defence and he had been against their marriage.

Marriage? Had it accomplished anything, this marriage of theirs? It certainly brought no easing of the sadness Rick's death had left on her heart. There had been no overwhelming thrill of revenge justly meted out. And what of Shiloh's reason for marrying her? It crossed her mind that his reason for marrying her had really rebounded on him. If the marriage had broken up before it began then wouldn't that only add to the intensity of the rumours about him?

Her tears fell again and she recalled the emotion-charged look that had passed between them at the reception. There could have been so much love . . . A sob caught in her throat. Yes, no matter what, she was in love with Shiloh, desperately, and the thought of life without him was suddenly unimaginable, a deep and aching void within her, and she yearned to feel his arms about her again. Would he be prepared to discuss their differences, attempt to make a go of their marriage? Could they put the past behind them?

It was worth a try. She would telephone him immediately. She stood up and walked towards the phone and then stopped just as suddenly. She didn't know his number, or even where he was. In fact she had no way of knowing where to contact him and she shrank from asking his parents. She would just have to wait until Shiloh got in contact with her and then she must hope she could find some way to convince him that it was only the future that mattered.

But Shiloh didn't phone or write, and Danni went off to work on Thursday, sick at heart and dreading Lisa's well-meaning questions about her newly married bliss.

She managed to carry it all off, but with each day that passed something inside her died just a little.

CHAPTER NINE

'THERE he is now,' said Jock Mathieson, moving off towards the conspicuous fiery red head of Dallas Byrne, who was weaving his way impatiently through the throng of people scurrying about the huge airport.

'Hi, Jock—Danni! Sorry I'm late. The traffic coming in was atrocious.' Dallas's eyes didn't meet Danni's as he took her small suitcase from her and turned to lead them outside to the car park. 'It made me feel like a real country bumpkin. Makes you wonder if there isn't more racing done off the track!'

They moved towards the escalators with the other travellers.

'Everything's ready out at the track. The car's spot on and ready to go. Your heats aren't until two-thirty, so there's no rush to get back. We can take our time, and drop your things off at the motel on the way.' Dallas stopped beside a pale blue sedan.

'Where's the utility?' asked Danni, looking about for their old grey truck.

'Oh, I didn't bring the ute. We're travelling with a little more class today.' Dallas was unlocking the boot of the new Ford. 'I ran into Shiloh this morning,' he explained, his ears pink, obviously embarrassed, 'and he insisted I use his sedan to collect you.'

'Where ... where did you see Shiloh?' Danni tried to keep her voice on an even keel while her heart was beating its own tattoo. Just the sound of his name made her senses reel alarmingly, and she could feel her father's eyes on her.

'At the track.' Dallas's voice was muffled as he bent over the boot, stowing Jock's case next to Danni's. 'He'd had his new car on the track for a practice run this morning. I've got to hand it to him,' his voice was gruff, 'it's a real beauty. His heats are just after yours this afternoon and it appears he'll be giving the boys a run for their money, going by his efforts this morning.'

Danni could only stare uncomprehendingly at Dallas's back while she fought to regain her composure after the shock she had received at Dallas's words. She knew her face was pale and she leant thankfully against the back of the car, her mind spinning with a jumble of thoughts.

'What heats are you talking about, Dallas?' Jock voiced the question that was uppermost in Danni's mind, a question she was at that moment totally incapable of asking. And when her father would have looked across at Danni, Dallas straightened up between them and turned to Jock.

'Formula 5000. He's having another go at the series.' Dallas slammed the boot. 'Chris Damien's backing him, although why . . .'

'What's all this, Danni?' Jock stepped aside so that he could direct his question at his daughter, a frown deep on his face. 'How can Shiloh race with his leg? It's suicide! Don't tell me you go along with this foolishness, Danni?'

'I . . .' Danni shrugged. 'It's . . . I guess it's something he feels he has to do,' she said lamely, using Shiloh's answer to his own father, her heart contracting at the thought of Shiloh racing again.

Dallas gave her a thoughtful look, although he made no comment, and Danni climbed into the back of the car before either of the men could see the trembling that had overcome her.

They were all strangely silent on the journey out to the race track and even Dallas seemed loath to discuss Danni's car, the racing competition or various bits of racing news he had picked up at the track, as he was wont to do. Danni herself was lost deeply in her own thoughts.

So there had been some truth in the newspaper report. He must have teamed up with Chris Damien. Why hadn't Shiloh mentioned his intention to race again so soon? This must have been the reason behind his father's anger. He had thought that Danni knew all about it, condoned it. And surely she had had a right to know his intention, especially before they were married? And what was more important, how could he even contemplate racing again after such an horrific accident and all that came after it? Unbidden, her mind visualised Shiloh lying limply in a twisted wreck, and she closed her eyes weakly, biting her lip so that she didn't cry out.

Her father shifted stiffly in his seat beside Dallas and Danni's eyes opened and rested on the back of his head, taking in the weather-roughened skin and the thinning grey hair.

Her father hadn't planned on coming along with her to the southern races, but at the last minute he had announced his intention to do so. Danni was sure he knew there was something amiss between her and Shiloh, but he had made no comment as yet. In a moment of revelation her heart went out to him. Was this how her father had felt when Rick had been competing? And did he experience this same churning dread each time she took to the track? It was such food for thought that Danni had to drag her mind back to the present when Dallas stopped the car and held her door open for her to climb out.

As usual Dallas had everything arranged and under control. All the paperwork was completed and Danni's Formula Ford was parked under a tarpaulin strung from the utility in a makeshift shelter from the sun. Yet even in the shade, the car shone brightly from a vigorous polishing. For the first time in her life Danni viewed the racing car with a feeling almost akin to revulsion.

'I'll make a pot of tea,' said Jock, unlocking the door of the small camping unit that was resting on the back tray of the utility.

Dallas's inevitable cloth was wiping away an imaginary smudge from the bodywork of the car while Danni stood as if in a trance, not hearing the general babble of voices raised above the throb of burbling engines, not noticing the comings and goings of drivers, mechanics and officials.

Setting her bag containing her driving suit almost unconsciously on the grass by her side, she continued to look at the car as it took on a terrifying shape, became an object of death and carnage, and her knees began to tremble. She clasped her dampened hands together and tried to suppress the shudder that threatened to pass over the length of her body. When a strong hand rested lightly on her shoulder she started violently, one hand going to her mouth, her eyes widening in fright.

'Sorry, I didn't mean to startle you, Danni.' The owner of the deep voice smiled crookedly. 'You must have been miles away.' Shiloh's cold tawny eyes flicked over to Dallas who stood watching them, his face set and grim. 'Thinking about me, I suppose.' Shiloh's smile didn't reach his eyes as he pulled Danni's numb body to him, his lips descending until they moved gently on hers.

Her lips opened, partly in surprise, partly in an involuntary pleasure and, at her trembling response, he pulled her closer, his kiss deepening until Danni clung to his broad shoulders for support. Shiloh raised his head, his eyes looking mockingly into hers.

'Now that's what I call the perfect wifely welcome.' His voice dropped lower, for her ears only. 'Or maybe it's just another of your little lead-them-round-on-a-leash tricks? Dare I surmise that you missed me, Mrs O'Rourke?'

Only Danni was aware of the underlying sarcasm in those last two words, and she felt her colour rise at the implications behind his cynical tone. As he continued to look at her lines of strain became etched around his lips and his hand moved caressingly along the length of her backbone, almost as though he couldn't help himself, and his half smile was self-derisive.

'Shiloh O'Rourke,' a petulant husky voice broke the thread of heightened tension between them, 'I let you out of my sight for a moment and where do I find you? In the arms of another woman!' Almond green eyes roved over Danni from top to toe, and the fact that the other girl found Danni wanting was quite obvious. It was there on her face, in the condescending twist of the reddened lips and the tilt of her perfect nose.

Danni recognised her immediately from the photo in the newspaper and she watched Shiloh's smile broaden, his expression relax, and, to Danni's chagrin, his not inconsiderable charm flow, as though the other girl's presence had turned on a tap. 'I always told you I was a two-timer,' he laughed. 'Anyway, Marla, Chris, come and meet my wife.'

Danni had to give the other girl her due, she took what was obviously a shock remarkably well, and only after she had noticed the slight flickering of the other girl's eyelashes and the aggressive light in the perfectly shaped eyes at Shiloh's shock statement did Danni notice that Marla Damien was accompanied by her husband. In fact, in a crowd, Chris Damien could be very easily overlooked for all that his name was well known in business and sporting circles. He was of medium height and build with mousey brown hair, already thinning, although he was only in his late thirties, and he had one of the plainest, kindest faces Danni had seen anywhere.

But Shiloh's arm about her waist was drawing her possessively against his side. 'Danni, this is Marla and Chris Damien.'

'You didn't mention that you were married, Shiloh, you secretive devil!' Marla's lip pouted, but her eyes flashed as she turned her attention to Danni. 'You don't look old enough to be married to anyone, let alone the dashing Shiloh O'Rourke.'

'We've only been married a short time. A week, in fact,' grinned Shiloh easily, 'so maybe Danni hasn't had time to look harassed.'

Marla's eyes ran suggestively over Danni's trim figure. 'Rather a sudden decision?' She turned back to Shiloh.

'A little, perhaps,' he replied goodnaturedly. 'You could say it was a case of love at first sight and once we'd made up our minds we couldn't see any sense in waiting, could we, darling?' His fingers tightened on Danni's waist.

'No sense at all,' Danni smiled sweetly at Shiloh and then at Marla and her husband. 'I thought it a good idea to get the knot safely tied,' Danni's blue eyes held Marla's, 'while he was still interested.' She watched the stiffening of the other girl's features.

'Now, that's funny. I was thinking the same thoughts about you,' replied Shiloh, taking the conversation in his stride.

'Congratulations anyway, mate,' Chris Damien spoke for the first time, holding his hand out to Shiloh. 'I hope you'll both be very happy. And nice to meet you, Danni.' He frowned thoughtfully. 'I seem to think we've met before somewhere.'

'We have,' Danni smiled genuinely, 'in Brisbane about eighteen months ago. My brother, Rick Mathieson, introduced us before a meeting at Lakeside.'

'Rick ... That's right. Danni Mathieson. Of course, I remember now. Rick's young sister.' He shook his head. 'Tragic time for us all.' He glanced sideways at his wife. 'You remember Rick Mathieson, dear?' he asked guardedly.

'So you're the kid sister Rick always talked about,' said Marla. 'I somehow always got the impression that you were still at school.' Marla's glance implied that Danni's appearance didn't alter that impression at all.

'It was my similar mistake that first had those beautiful blue eyes flashing at me.' Shiloh planted an affectionate kiss on the end of Danni's nose just as Jock's head appeared around the door of the van.

The conversation flowed about Danni without any sense of reality. The only tangible thing was Shiloh's hand resting on her waist, his strong firm muscles moving against her, setting her physically aflame, coupled with the barely disguised anger in Marla Damien's eyes.

'It's just about time to get ready, Danni.' Dallas had walked up to them and stood on the outskirts, almost an outsider, a tense frown on his face as his gaze settled on Danni and Shiloh.

Disentangling herself from Shiloh's arm, Danni made the introductions, watching distastefully as Marla Damien's eyes moved speculatively over Dallas. 'Would you excuse me, I have to change for my heats.'

'My, my, you do have hidden talents, Danni!' purred Marla Damien.

'And some not so hidden,' laughed Shiloh as Danni moved thankfully over to the van.

By the time she returned only her father and Dallas were standing by the car.

'Shiloh said he'd see you after the race,' her father told her, his eyes moving from Danni's figure clad in her bright safety suit to the racing car. 'I'll head off over to the grandstand and get a good seat. Good luck, love.' He touched Danni on the arm and walked off towards the track.

Danni watched him anxiously, lost in thought, her heart going out to her father. Dallas had to wave his hand in front of her to get her attention.

'Hey, Danni, snap out of it!' He handed her her balaclava and she tucked her hair inside it before looking at him. His face was creased with a worried frown, as though he had been reading her thoughts. For those few moments she had been on the verge of withdrawing from the race and she knew by the look on Dallas's face that he suspected as much.

'It's all right, Dallas. I'm ready.' Before she could think she climbed into the car, strapping her safety helmet in place and adjusting her harness. Her mind was numb, so much so that she was on the track before she surfaced from the dull nothingness of her thoughts. Her hands tightened on the wheel and she could feel the perspiration breaking out on her brow. Her heartbeats quickened as a never before experienced fear washed over her in a wave of uncertainty. She'd never felt anything like this before, not even in her first race. Had she lost her nerve?

Dallas was waiting as Danni swung the Formula Ford under the tarpaulin and killed the engine. His eyes followed her every movement as she removed her helmet and balaclava and shook out her damp hair.

'What happened?' he asked eventually. 'Was it the car?'

Danni shrugged. 'No, it wasn't the car. That was perfect as always. It was me. I just—I don't know, I just couldn't get into the action.'

Dallas shook his head. 'You'll be in the middle of the pack tomorrow.'

'I know.' Danni pulled off her gloves. 'I'm . . . I'm sorry, Dallas. I have a headache. I think I'll have a rest in the van.'

'Aren't you coming across to watch the rest of the races?'

'No. No, you go, Dallas. I'll see you later.' Danni stepped into the van and slowly peeled off her racing suit. She splashed her hot face with tepid water and climbed into a pair of jeans and a loose, sleeveless top. Lying down on one of the bunks, she closed her eyes, wishing fervently that she could close her mind as easily.

What was the matter with her anyway? So Shiloh was racing again. So what? That was his business. If he chose to kill himself then . . . Danni pressed her hand to her mouth, a feeling of nausea rising within her. She couldn't explain this crushing fear. Even when Rick was racing she hadn't suffered more than a slight uneasiness.

She lay on the bunk, her thoughts chaotic, until her father's voice brought the realisation that the shadows in the van had deepened.

'Danni? You there, love?'

'Yes, Pop, I'm here.' She struggled off the bunk as her father opened the door and poked his head inside. 'I must have dozed off.'

'Pity you didn't come over to the track. Shiloh did pretty well in his heats. He'll be on the front line tomorrow,' Jock said, carefully not mentioning Danni's race. 'Not that I agree with him going back to racing, especially the 5000's,' he began, and broke off. 'Yes, well, it's none of my business, I guess.'

'Where's Dallas?' Danni changed the subject.

'He's met up with some mates and will probably spend the evening with them. We're going to have a slap-up dinner at the motel restaurant and if we head off now it'll give you time to get yourself prettied up,' he grinned.

'I've only brought one dress with me, Pop,' Danni began, 'and it's hardly suitable to dine in style.'

'You'd look beautiful in a sack, love,' laughed her father. 'Now come on, I've booked a table.'

When Danni emerged from their motel room a short time later her father had gone, and her step faltered when she recognised the broad shoulders of the man standing waiting for her. As she pulled the door to, his eyes moved over her figure in the long patterned hostess dress.

'Where's my father?' she asked, trying to appear as calm as he looked.

'Gone over to the restaurant.' Shiloh shoved his hands deep into the pockets of his dark brown slacks, drawing her attention to the latent strength in his muscular thighs. There was no denying his attractiveness with his cream short-sleeved body shirt moulding the muscular contours of his chest and shoulders and his fair hair lifting in the cool breeze of dusk, highlighted by the fluorescent lights. 'You didn't do so well today.'

'No.' Danni felt her hackles begin to rise and took a steadying breath. 'There's always tomorrow,' she tried to be offhand. Trust him to get her back up before the evening began!

He was regarding her with his tawny eyes. 'Any troubles mechanically?'

'None. There never is.' Danni's reply was terse. 'Dallas is an A grade mechanic. I just wasn't firing,' she shrugged.

'You shouldn't go out on the track if you aren't mentally and physically pitched to compete.'

'I shouldn't go out on the track? That's rich!' Danni's body tensed. 'And you, of course, are in perfect physical condition, I suppose.'

'We weren't talking about me,' he said clippedly.

'No, you weren't. But I am. You failed to mention your intention to continue motor racing so soon. I had to find out from Dallas this afternoon.' Danni's anger blazed. 'How do you think I felt, having to pretend I knew all about it?'

'Don't tell me you cared?' Sarcasm put an edge to his voice. 'I might be led to believe that you've reconsidered your childish ...'

'Oh, what's the use?' Danni cut him off and went to swing away from him, but his hand grasped her wrist, forcing her back to him, her eyes meeting his, and alarm overrode her anger at the fierceness of his expression. Their eyes locked and duelled, Danni knowing he would always have the upper hand, and with a muffled curse he drew her against him, crushing her lips beneath his.

Danni tried to free herself from the havoc he was wreaking upon her, knowing how easily she could be seduced by his assault upon her senses. Her hand on his chest registered the racing of his heart as it pounded his arousal.

Eventually Shiloh dragged his lips from hers and his breathing was fast and irregular. 'Danni, I ...' He shook his head, part in anger, part in exasperation. 'God, I can't take much more of this. As you said, "What's the bloody use?" Let's go and have dinner.'

The restaurant was relatively crowded and Jock welcomed them without noticing the unleashed charge of electricity which still sparked between them. The meal was delicious and Danni made a pretence of enjoying it, although every mouthful tasted like ashes. The men didn't appear to notice that she added little to the conversation, wrapped as they were in their own discussion of the day's heats and tomorrow's races. Any antagonism between them seemed to have been shelved for the evening.

They were drinking a cup of coffee after their meal when Jock's words brought Danni's head up in shock. Passing the key to their motel room across to Shiloh, he said casually, 'You may as well stay here with Danni. I'll bunk down in the van with Dallas.'

'Pop, you can't!' The words broke from Danni in dismay. 'You and I were going to share the motel room, and besides, the van's far too cramped for you,' she added lamely.

'Rubbish!' said Jock. 'I've slept in tighter spots,' he grinned.

'But ...' she appealed to Shiloh with her eyes as he sat back smiling a trifle tensely.

'Very thoughtful of you, Jock. We'll take you up on that,' he replied easily. 'It saves me trying to convince Danni she should come down to my tent at the track.' He winked at his father-in-law. 'This is a much better arrangement.'

Jock laughed and set his empty cup on its saucer. 'Well, I'll leave you to it. You can bring Danni back in your car in the morning, okay?' He bent to kiss Danni lightly on the forehead. 'See you tomorrow, love.'

'Thanks, Jock.' Shiloh smiled with general bonhomie.

Danni fixed her gaze on the dregs in the coffee cup she clenched in her hand, refusing to look at Shiloh.

After a moment he stood up and walked around to the back of her chair. 'Come on, Danni. I want to get an early night tonight.'

Danni stood up stiffly. 'If you think ...' she began.

'Save it, Danni,' he bit off between clenched teeth, 'unless you want to make a scene right here in the middle of the restaurant.'

His fingers firmly held her upper arm as they walked across to their room. Unlocking the door, he all but shoved Danni inside and flicked on the lights.

As motel rooms went it passed muster, although at that moment Danni was totally unaware of the décor. To one side was a double bed and on the other a narrow single divan with matching olive green quilts. There was the usual bench for suitcases, a television set and a small refrigerator and a door led off to the small bathroom and toilet.

Danni swung around as Shiloh slammed the door and leant back against it with his arms folded, and her eyes flashed darkly with suppressed anger. 'I'm not staying here with you and that's final,' she stated, with more conviction than she actually felt.

'Quit playing the outraged maiden, Danni,' he said flatly, moving towards her as he pulled off his body shirt.

Danni drew back instinctively, but he was heading for the bathroom.

'There are two beds. I'm taking the double, so you can have your choice.' He tossed his shirt on the bed. 'Has Jock left his shaving gear here? Ah, yes.' He rubbed his hand over his jaw as he picked up the electric shaver. 'I could use a shave and a shower.'

He disappeared into the bathroom while Danni's eyes followed him, watching the play of light on his broad muscular shoulders which had grown tanned in the few weeks since they had swum together at his parents' home. Was it only weeks ago? It seemed an age.

Danni glanced towards the outer door and had taken a few steps towards it before she realised the futility of it. Where could she go? With the motor races being held this weekend all the accommodation nearby would be taken. Sighing, she walked across and removed her cotton nightdress and robe from her overnight case and sat down wearily on the single bed.

When Shiloh appeared he had a towel wrapped loosely around him, hanging low on his narrow hips, and Danni's eyes moved over his body, almost hypnotised by its firmness, glistening with dampness. But he barely glanced in her direction, simply folding his slacks over a hanger and stowing them in a cupboard.

'The shower's free,' he said without turning around.

Danni stood up and walked towards the door.

'You might as well take this towel in with you,' he said as she passed him and, to her consternation, he unwrapped it from his waist and put it into her hands.

Danni flushed scarlet, turning quickly from his naked body, and his teasing chuckle followed her into the bathroom until she closed the door on the taunting sound. She spent a considerable time under the shower, trying to relax her tension-stretched muscles and, somewhat reluctantly, in some trepidation she slowly opened the door.

To her surprise the room was in semi-darkness. Only the small lamp by the television set emitted a subdued glow and Shiloh's still form was spread out on the double bed, his face to the wall, the bottom half of his body covered by the light cream sheet. She listened intently to his relaxed breathing, realising he was already asleep. Moving quietly so as not to disturb him, she crossed to the single divan and turned down the covers before switching off the lamp and slipping between the sheets.

She lay tense and stiff staring into the darkness, her hearing tuned to Shiloh's even breathing, knowing she was far too alert to even contemplate sleep. Unbidden came the thought that she could very well have slipped into the bed beside Shiloh. In fact, part of her wished she could do just that, wished she had the nerve to get up from the confines of this narrow uncomfortable divan and feel the length of his body alongside hers. No doubt, given the chance, Marla Damien would have had no hesitation in doing so. For all Danni knew she could already have ...

A pain somewhere in the vicinity of her heart made her close her eyes at the realisation that she was burningly jealous of the other girl's relationship with Shiloh. She shut her mind to Marla Damien, tried to blot out that photograph in the newspaper. She had no proof that Shiloh was in any way involved with her. Besides, Marla was married to the very nice, very rich Chris Damien.

Eventually Danni must have slipped into a troubled sleep, although it seemed to be only a few minutes before she stirred. Something, some noise, had woken her. Danni stared into the gloom, the darkness broken intermittently by the pale glow of a flashing neon sign.

When the babble of incoherent words broke the quietness Danni almost jumped out of her skin. Her fingers clutched the sheets, her heart pounding loudly in her ears. She realised the sound was coming from the double bed and she sat up as Shiloh began to toss about, his voice rising a shade higher.

Was he ill? Without thinking she was out of bed and had padded across the room, flicking on the reading lamp over his bed and standing looking down at him. He began muttering again, a jumble of words, none of which she could catch. He must be dreaming, not pleasantly, judging by the agitated way he was thrashing about.

Danni's hand went out to wake him when he began moving about with more violence, throwing his arms up to protect his face, and then his hands went to move agitatedly over his legs. He began talking again and this time his words were painfully

clear. 'I'm caught. Can't move. Have to get out.
Get me out! His voice rose.

Kneeling on the side of the bed, Danni tried to
wake him as gently as she could, and his skin was
damp to touch. In the light from the reading lamp
she could see beads of perspiration on his brow. He
surfaced slowly from the depths of obvious terror into
which his subconscious had lured him while he slept.
His eyes opened and he took some time to focus on
her worried face.

'Danni?' His yellow eyes were vulnerable for a
split second as they questioningly searched her face.

'I'm sorry I had to wake you,' Danni said quickly.
'You were calling out in your sleep. You were
having a nightmare.' She stood back off the bed as
he ran a shaky hand over his damp face. Tendrils of
damp hair clung to his forehead.

'I'll get you a towel.' She disappeared into the
bathroom, returning with a dampened flannel and a
fresh towel. His eyes were closed again and she bent
over him, sponging his face and chest, trying not to
allow her eyes to move downwards to where the sheet
had fallen low on his hips.

Levering himself up, Shiloh took the towel from
her and wiped himself dry while Danni filled a glass
with water and passed it to him. He downed it
thirstily and grimaced. 'I guess I was yelling a bit,'
he remarked, looking at her warily. 'Did I say
anything?'

'You were mumbling incoherently and thrashing
about,' she said simply. 'Have you had these dreams
before?'

'Once or twice. In the beginning.' He threw the
towel on to a chair and sighed. 'I haven't had one in
months.' Silence lay between them for a few seconds.

'Sorry I woke you up.' He flexed his shoulders stiffly.

'That's all right. Will you be able to sleep now? I mean, do you ... do you need anything else? More water? A cup of coffee?'

He shook his head slightly and the spark of electricity that had burned between them earlier in the evening suddenly flared to mammoth proportions.

'Well, I'll get back to bed.' Danni's heart seemed to beat in her throat.

'There is something else I need,' he said softly. 'You.' His hand went out to her wrist, his eyes setting a trail of molten fire from her lips, to the pulse beating at the base of her throat lower to the rise and fall of her breasts outlined beneath the thin cotton of her nightdress.

Danni's heart was racing and her mouth had gone dry. She was suddenly incapable of making a move to break the hold he had on her.

'Danni.' His voice was low and husky, sending vibrations through her entire body. 'Don't go.' His hand on her wrist pulled her down to him.

Danni knew she should resist, knew he would let her go if she pulled back, but did she want to? Wasn't this exactly what she had wanted right from the beginning? Her eyes were enmeshed in the web of desire that spread from the depths of his, their tawniness flowing through her like molten gold, his pupils diluted in his heightened arousal.

Gentle hands pulled her down on top of him and, as they lay length to length, his lips found hers, moving sensuously, each moment drawing her further away from the realms of conscious thought. In that moment, the past didn't matter, held no meaning. There was only the present, now, with

Shiloh's lips on hers, his body pressed against every responding inch of her own.

Her senses, her mind, her whole body reacted to his aroused maleness and she knew she could welcome drowning in the ecstasy of his kisses and caresses. His hands moved over the contours of her body beneath the thin cotton that separated them and soon her nightdress became a barrier, an object that sought to keep their straining bodies apart.

Shiloh's strong arms lifted her and then she was lying in his arms, their bodies free, skin upon skin, as close as two people can ever be. The burning touch of his body against hers made coherent thought an impossibility. Shiloh's hand moved over her hips, up to her breast, covering its taut arousal and, as his lips moved down to replace his hand, Danni moaned softly, yielding to his touch, her fingers twining in the soft fairness of his hair.

'Mmm. You're more beautiful than I imagined.' His voice was thick with heightened passion. 'God, Danni, I want you so much!'

'Shiloh.' Danni's voice was faintly slurred through the fullness of her swollen lips, still throbbing from his kisses. 'We shouldn't ...'

His firm body moved incredibly closer, one leg imprisoning hers, and she trembled with renewed awareness of his male hardness. His lips moved back to the hollow of her throat and up to tease her ear-lobe. 'You want me too, Danni.' His lips trailed along the line of her jaw to the jut of her chin. 'Don't stop me now,' he murmured huskily, 'because I somehow don't think I can.' And his lips covered hers, demanding a spontaneous response which she met with a passion to equal his ...

Danni struggled through waves of sleep, wondering vaguely why there was a pinning weight lying across her body, preventing her from movement. She stirred in protest, turning her head on the pillow, her eyelids fluttering and then opening wide at the sight of Shiloh's fair head resting heavily against her shoulder.

Her body flushed at the intimacy of their position and the events of the night before came back to her in vivid detail. Her first instinct was to push herself away from him, put as much distance as possible between them, but how could the blame for what had happened be laid singly on either of them? Their lovemaking had been so right, something they had both wanted, needed, something neither of them could deny.

She smiled to herself, a little flutter of love stirring delightfully within her. Of its own will her hand went up to smooth his sleep-tossled hair. It looked as untidy as it had the first afternoon she had met him on the practice track at Mallaroo. Her fingers moved caressingly from his hair over his slightly roughened cheek, where his fair lashes rested in a peaceful curve, down to his firm jawline, one finger coming to rest against his lips.

He stirred and smiled sleepily, his arms drawing her closer. 'If I'm dreaming all this, don't dare wake me up to tell me,' he murmured, his lips brushing her tautening nipple. 'Mmm, you're a witch, Mrs O'Rourke, do you know that?' His lips sought hers and once again they arched together in their mutual arousal.

When the telephone jangled loudly, it was some time before the sound penetrated their private rapture.

'Shouldn't we answer the phone?' Danni murmured.

'Should we?' he teased, his lips following the swell of her breast.

'It might be important,' Danni tried again without a lot of conviction.

'So it might,' he grinned ruefully, one hand groping for the receiver, winking at her as he held it to her ear.

'Hello,' Danni blushed as Shiloh's lips renewed their teasing trail.

'Who is that?' The silky feminine voice was immediately recognisable.

'Danni O'Rourke. What can I do for you, Mrs Damien?' Danni felt Shiloh's caresses cease and he raised himself on one elbow, watching Danni's face.

'Nothing, thank you,' Marla's tone was all condescension. 'Actually I wanted to speak to Shiloh. Jock, your father, gave me this number. Do you know where I can reach him?'

Danni suppressed a desire to giggle hysterically. 'Yes, he's here. But he's just a little busy at the moment,' she said wickedly. 'However, I'll put him on.'

Shiloh's fair eyebrow rose as he took the phone. 'Shiloh O'Rourke here.'

Danni watched his profile as he listened to the other girl.

'Are you sure he needs me right away? I understood we weren't due at the track until ten o'clock.' He listened for a moment, a frown puckering his brow. 'All right, I'll be there as soon as I can.' Letting the receiver fall back on to the cradle, he looked ruefully at Danni, his eyes lingering on the contours of her body.

'I had a feeling we should have ignored that damn phone,' he said gruffly, his hand moving to her body as though he was unable to stop himself.

When she thought he would have said to heck with the phone call he dragged himself away from her and walked into the bathroom. Danni sat up, wrapping the sheet around her.

'Why do you have to go out to the track so early?' she called after him.

'Marla didn't have any details.'

'Oh.' Danni pulled a face. Marla Damien spoke and Shiloh jumped. She sat and mulled over that thought.

Shiloh's head appeared around the door. 'Danni, I'm sorry I can't stay, but Chris wouldn't call me out if it wasn't important.'

They looked at each other and Shiloh shook his head, reaching for his clothes. 'Are you coming with me?'

'I guess. If you want me to,' she replied flatly.

'That's not the point. Look, I'll send the car back for you. How about nine-thirty?'

'Shiloh?' Danni's voice halted him by the door. 'Do you ... must you race?' she asked softly.

He ran a hand through his hair. 'God, Danni, this is hardly the time to start on that. You know how it is? I'm not asking *you* to give up racing.' He spoke as though she dabbled in the sport as a hobby, like oil-painting. 'Look, I've got to go,' he glanced at his wristwatch. 'I owe Chris Damien quite a lot for taking me on.' The door closed and he had gone.

CHAPTER TEN

'HEY, Danni, where are you going?' Dallas looked up from the engine of the yellow Formula Ford.

'Just across to the other pits. Won't be long.'

'You race in twenty minutes.'

'I know that, Dallas,' Danni replied shortly. 'I'll be back in time.'

She had been at the track for over four hours and she hadn't set eyes on Shiloh. Something deep inside her drove her towards the pits where the Formula 5000's were preparing for their race later in the afternoon. She wanted to see him before she went on the track, although she refused to acknowledge that she needed anything as basic as reassurance from him.

His distinctive black and pale blue Formula 5000 was easy to find and there were quite a number of interested fans milling about the racing car under the watchful gaze of two overalled mechanics. Shiloh was nowhere to be seen, so Danni approached one of the mechanics and was directed to a tent nearby.

The much trampled grass softened her footfalls as she neared the tent, and it wasn't until she was about to slip under the overhanging awning that she recognised Marla Damien's voice. She stopped in her tracks as she caught the other girl's words.

'Darling, you look so attractive in your racing suit and I'm sure you're going to show them your dust if the heats are anything to go by. You were absolutely fantastic! It was just so exciting watching you drive.'

'Thanks, Marla, for the ego boost,' there was amusement in Shiloh's voice, 'and as to the race—well, we'll see.'

Marla laughed huskily. 'You know, you're too modest, darling. None of those drivers out there can match you in technique and they know it.'

Shiloh laughed shortly. 'And you don't think old Lady Luck plays any part in it?'

Realising she was eavesdropping, Danni felt decidedly foolish and moved again towards the tent opening.

'We make our own luck.' Marla's voice had dropped a shade lower. 'And I somehow have a feeling you're going to be one of the winners.'

'I lost last time I raced.' Shiloh's voice didn't seem to hold any anger. 'You didn't lose any time getting out then.' It was as though he was discussing something as mundane as the weather.

'What was a girl to do?' Marla said huskily.

'What indeed?' Shiloh gave a laugh. 'I don't suppose giving a little moral support crossed your mind.'

'You're a bastard, Shiloh O'Rourke. Perhaps that's why I'm so crazy about you.'

'Dare I remind you about Chris?' Shiloh's voice now contained a sharp edge.

'Chris was there when I needed him,' said Marla, 'but now that you're back—well . . .'

'I'm back to race.'

Marla laughed in her throat, causing a shiver of revulsion to pass over Danni. 'And I know you're going to win this time.' Her tone was an implication in itself. 'Chris has every faith in you. But just in case, to cover all exits, I don't think a kiss for the very best of luck would be out of order, do you?'

Danni stood transfixed in the tent opening, watching Marla's red-tipped fingers move in Shiloh's fair hair, almost the same way that Danni's fingers had moved through his hair that morning. Pain rose from deep within her and, as Shiloh's hands went to the other girl's waist, Danni must have made some involuntary sound, because Shiloh's eyes turned and locked with hers.

Marla Damien was a little slower to react and when she turned to face Danni there was a certain flash of smugness reflected in her almond eyes. Swinging on her heel and ignoring Shiloh's call after her, Danni all but ran back to the van where Dallas was pacing nervously up and down.

'Good grief, Danni, you're sure cutting it fine,' he said tersely, reaching for her helmet. 'Are you okay? You look a bit pale.'

'I'm fine, Dallas. Don't fuss. Let's get on to the track.'

She sat on the starting grid, the vibrating throb of the engine about her, her body seemingly a thing apart from her mind. There were seven cars in front of her, but at that particular moment she was totally oblivious to their shape or their sound.

At least now she knew where she stood. God, what a fool she was! Shiloh had made no secret of the fact that he had wanted her, desired her physically, right from the start, and now he had had what he wanted. Like a lovesick fool she had fallen into his arms, ripe for the picking. And he had gone straight from her bed at a word from Marla Damien and ended up in her arms.

Squeezing her eyes closed, she tried to blot out the picture of the two of them that seemed to be stained on her mind. When she opened her eyes the track was cleared and the starter stood poised on his stand. She must force it all to the back of her mind, think about it later. For now, the race needed all her concentration. But one thing was for sure, Shiloh O'Rourke would not get the chance to humiliate her again, she promised herself that. He wouldn't get close enough.

The flag fell and with grim cold resolution Danni left twin black ribbons on the asphalt behind her.

Dallas helped her out of the car and for once he was speechless. She removed her helmet and looked at his startled face.

'Well, Dallas, our first win,' she said, her senses still high with exhilaration and just a little shocked dismay.

'God, Danni! You just took ten years off my life,' Dallas burst out. 'What, by all that's holy, came over you? I've never seen you drive like that, so . . . so . . .' He lifted his hands and let them fall in bewilderment.

'Singlemindedly?' She raised her eyebrows.

In all honesty she couldn't explain to herself what had come over her. Up till now she would have described herself as a defensive rather than an aggressive driver, but today she had driven like a fiend, taking chances she could even now scarcely believe she had taken. Oh, she had always driven to win, but . . .

Pushing these thoughts aside, she looked up at her mechanic. 'How about some congratulations instead of that long face, Dallas? I would have thought you would be delighted.'

'Well, I am. But ... God, Danni! What made you
...?' The fact that Dallas was swearing said much
for his distress.

'There's no pleasing you, Dallas Byrne.' Suddenly
the whole thing had gone flat. She wanted to be
alone, alone to come to terms with the reactions that
were beginning to set in. Her legs felt rubbery, as
though they were about to give way beneath her, and
she turned to walk around to the door of the van to
change her clothes, to sit down before she fell down.

She had begun the race half way down the field of
starters and from there had worked her way to the
lead through sheer determination, pushing herself
and the car to the limit, outmanoeuvring the drivers
in front of her, to take the race on the last straight
by half a car's length, oblivious to the roaring excitement of the crowd. Now, as she looked back, it
seemed as though a demon had been driving her,
pushing her, forcing her onwards. And she, before
anyone else, realised the danger, the foolhardiness in
that.

She had only taken two steps towards the van
when her arm was seized in a punishing grip and
she was wrenched around to face a tall livid figure.

'Just what the hell was that supposed to prove?'
Shiloh's voice was deceptively low, the words forced
out between lips tight with anger.

'Shiloh, you're ... you're hurting me!' She tried
to pull her wrist from the pain of his grasp.

'Hurting you? I should take a strap to you! It
would be a fraction of what you deserve after that
display of bloody stupidity!' His hands went to her
shoulders and he shook her until she thought she
would faint.

Dallas moved forward, putting a restraining hand

on Shiloh's arm. 'That's enough, O'Rourke. This isn't going to accomplish anything.'

Dallas's words stilled Shiloh's hands, but he didn't even glance at the other man. 'Keep out of this, Byrne. It's between Danni and me.'

'Look, I'm not going to stand by and let you ...'

'I said, keep out of it.' Shiloh's eyes flashed coldly as he pushed Danni towards the door of the van. 'My wife and I have things to discuss. Alone,' he finished pointedly.

Dallas took a step forward, but Danni shook her head, knowing Shiloh wouldn't hesitate to knock him down. She almost fell up the steps, propelled by Shiloh's strong arm, and as he slammed the door closed behind him she turned on him, preparing to do battle.

'Don't say a word.' He held his hand up. 'I've got things to say to you, and you're going to listen if I have to beat it into your spoilt little hide!'

'Shiloh, there's no need for all this ... this intensity,' Danni began.

'Intensity?' He looked as though he'd have liked to hit her and she took a step backwards. 'You know, you are one thoughtless, selfish little bitch!'

'Now wait a minute. Nobody calls me ...' she broke off as he advanced on her and she stepped back until her legs came up against the bunk.

'No, you wait a minute. I was sitting with your father during your race and I watched his face. While you played Stirling Moss I saw him age twenty years. Do you know what you're doing to him? You're tearing him apart, and I think it's about time someone put a stop to it.'

Danni's face had paled. For all her anger his words were hitting home. Wasn't he telling the truth? Wasn't she causing her father the agony he described? Her eyes dropped to the floor. Of course she was. A hundred times she had refused to acknowledge the flashes of worry on his face.

'I think the time has come for you to retire. And what better time than after such an amazing, showy performance? The fans will talk about it for years,' Shiloh said sarcastically.

'I'm not retiring, no matter what you say.' Danni's eyes flashed back. 'I admit I drove a little recklessly today, but—well, I'm going to win the Driver to Europe Competition. I'm in the lead on points now.' She looked at him defiantly.

'You are giving up motor racing,' his finger dug her shoulder as he emphasised each clipped word, 'as of now. Besides, you're going to be too busy in future, being my wife and a mother to my children.'

'That's the answer to everything as far as men are concerned, isn't it? Keep the little woman barefoot and pregnant. Well, I won't be dictated to by you or anyone else!'

Shiloh took one step forward and his thighs rested against hers. Blood pounded in her veins, her heartbeats skipping, as her traitorous body reacted to his touch, the sensations spreading like wildfire.

'I mean every word I've said, Danni. And on top of it all I don't think your father can take too much more of what you dished out today.'

'Pop's never said he wanted me to give up racing,' she began, the movement of his thighs setting her aflame.

'He shouldn't have to tell you, you should be able to see it on his face. You would if you thought about someone else's feelings instead of your own.' He glanced at his wristwatch. 'I have to go, I'm due on the track. We'll talk about it later tonight. But you may as well let the officials know that you're withdrawing from further competition.'

'I am not withdrawing,' she said firmly, 'and that's final.'

'We'll see about that. I'll take care of it myself.'

'Don't you dare!'

'And if I do?' he drawled tauntingly, his eyes moving down to the agitated rise and fall of her breasts beneath the enveloping driving suit. His fingers took hold of the zipper and pulled downwards. His eyes had changed colour, burning with a different emotion, and Danni raised her hands to his chest to fend him off. But her fingers settled caressingly on the thin material of his T-shirt and his lips descended on to hers. His hand had dragged the zipper to her waist and moved caressingly over her breast when a knock on the door of the van broke the bond of mutual arousal that had sprung between them.

'Shiloh? Danni? You in there?' Jock's voice called, and Shiloh reluctantly released her, pulling the opening of her suit back together and raising the zipper, smiling mockingly into her flushed face.

'Coming, Jock.' His eyes didn't leave Danni's face. 'I think I've proved my point, don't you?' he said softly before he went to the door. 'We'll talk later.'

However, Danni didn't stay to see Shiloh's race. All at once she couldn't bear to spend another moment at the race track. There were two vacant seats on an earlier flight, and when she told her father she intended to return home earlier than planned he decided to accompany her. Jock made no mention of Shiloh or the race as they winged their way northwards, and it wasn't until they sat over a cup of tea in the house at Broadbeach that he put his hand over one of hers and waited for her to look at him.

'Do you feel like talking about it, love?'

Danni had been holding it all inside and her father's sympathy broke the wall of the dam. She dissolved into his arms, sobbing brokenheartedly. Bit by bit the whole story came out, Danni telling her father far more than she realised she was, right down to the moment she had seen Marla Damien in Shiloh's arms.

'Oh, Pop, I'm sorry about the race today. I don't know why I drove like that. I must have given you a terrible time, but I was so upset and angry at . . . at everything.'

Jock looked down at her tear-filled eyes. 'By everything I guess you mean Shiloh?'

'Pop, he wants me to give up racing. In fact he ordered me to give it up, and I'm leading in points in the Driver to Europe Competition. You know how we always planned for me to be the first woman to take out the series.'

'You'll have to decide just how much it really, honestly means to you, which means the most to you, the competition, or Shiloh. Maybe to get a lot you'll have to give up a little.'

'But, Pop, no one's asking Shiloh to make that kind of decision!'

'Not that he realises, love, but during your race today, he suffered. Why do you think he was so angry? Maybe today he learned how hard it is to sit on the sidelines. Look, love, I don't deny that Rourkey was the last person I would have chosen for you, but I didn't realise until I saw his face as he watched you race just how much he cares for you,' Jock told her.

'Cares for me?' Danni sniffed. 'All he cares about is motor racing.' Marla Damien's face encroached on her memory, but she pushed it aside. 'Why else would he go back to it after it had nearly killed him?'

Jock shrugged his shoulders. 'Who knows? Didn't you tell me he feels he has something to prove to himself?'

They fell silent for a moment.

'How can you condone his racing after what happened to Rick, Pop?' Danni asked quietly. 'Especially when Shiloh was involved.'

Her father sighed heavily. 'Danni, Rick's death is something we have to learn to live with, and we owe it to Shiloh to put it behind us. When it happened I was angry, burning mad, and I wanted to blame someone for my hurt. I was open and waiting to believe someone had caused the accident when the rumours began, and I even believed it was Rourkey.'

'But if he was to blame ...' Danni broke in.

'No, love, I know now he wasn't,' Jock said sadly. 'I was talking to Chris Damien about it and he told me he'd seen an amateur movie of the race and it was a clear-cut blow-out of Don Christie's front tyre that moved him against the back of Shiloh's car. It was only a brilliant piece of driving on Shiloh's part as he tried to pull himself out of it that kept him out of the collision that followed. He very nearly pulled it off, too, according to Chris.'

'If ... Why didn't Shiloh tell everyone about the movie?' A pain clutched at Danni's heart. 'It would have cleared his name, stopped all the talk.'

'Maybe he thought it was best left.' Jock sighed. 'There's only pain in raking it all over. We know that, don't we, love?' He frowned worriedly. 'That's been the trouble between the two of you?' The question was almost a statement.

Danni sighed and shook her head, her mind and body exhausted. 'Yes and no, Pop. We should never have got married. I made a mistake. Maybe I'm just not the marrying kind.' She tried to lighten the conversation.

'What do you mean, not the marrying kind? That's utter nonsense and you know it,' stated her father. 'I think it's time you sat down together and talked all this out. Marriage is an all or nothing thing, love. You can't take it on and off like a coat.' He patted her hand. 'When Shiloh comes home tomorrow you talk it all out.'

But Shiloh didn't come home next morning. Dallas arrived back with Danni's car on Thursday, and it was from him that Danni learned that Shiloh had easily won his race at Sandown and had gone across to South Australia with Chris Damien to compete in an unscheduled race meeting to be held in Adelaide on the state's public holiday the following Monday.

Danni's heart sank to its lowest ebb, and by Sunday evening she thought she had never felt so lost and alone in her life. Her father had suggested she spend the weekend at Mallaroo, but she had declined, not wanting to have to pretend that everything was fine, that she didn't care that Shiloh had not even taken the trouble to call to let her know where he was. Now she half wished she had gone out to the Farm. Anything was better than sitting alone in this mood of cold despair.

When a car turned into the driveway at nine o'clock Danni closed her eyes, hoping it wasn't

Dallas. She couldn't bear to talk about anything to do with motor racing tonight, and Dallas was the last person she could talk to about Shiloh. At least she had been sitting in the dark, so if she stayed quiet perhaps her visitor would think she was having an early night or had gone out somewhere.

She listened as footsteps mounted the stairs and then a key clicked in the lock and the door swung open. It must be her father. Standing up, she flicked on the standard lamp, throwing the living-room into soft light.

'That you, Pop?'

There was no answer.

Something was dropped softly on to the hall carpet and then, as Danni stood transfixed, a tall figure appeared in the doorway.

Danni's heart leapt into her mouth, and as she recognised the thin features it crossed her mind that she might have preferred an intruder. 'You could have called out. You nearly frightened me to death!' Her defences were up again while her heart cried out at his nearness.

He smiled crookedly. 'That's what I like, an affectionate welcome from my ever-loving wife,' he remarked drily.

'What kind of welcome can you expect when you don't even let me know where you are?' Danni snapped back at him. This wasn't the way she had imagined his homecoming to be. It was all going so wrong. They just seemed to antagonise each other the moment they got together.

'I see. I should let you know my every movement, but you can leave the track without a whisper. That sounds fair,' he said sarcastically. 'Maybe I thought you needed time to come to your senses,' he added, tossing his keys on to the sideboard and walking across to pour himself a Scotch. 'Anyway,' he took a drink, 'I was sure the redoubtable Dallas would fill you in on my activities as soon as he got here.'

'He said you would be racing at Adelaide today and tomorrow.'

Shiloh emptied his glass in one gulp. 'I was. But I changed my mind.' He was looking down at his empty glass. 'Would you believe I wanted to see you?'

All of Danni's uncertainty and reaction to seeing him welled up inside her and she wanted him to feel some of the hurt she had suffered in the past week. 'I take it the lovely Marla was otherwise engaged?' Once the words were said Danni could feel horrified at her spitefulness, and only when Shiloh started angrily towards her did she retreat into her bedroom.

He was there before she could slam the door and he stood looking angrily at her. 'Not so very long ago if a wife behaved like a shrew her husband gave her a good hiding.'

'Shiloh, you wouldn't . . .'

He raised a sardonic eyebrow.

'If you come one step nearer I swear I'll . . . I'll . . .' Danni's step backwards was halted by the bed.

'You'll what? For a librarian you're surprisingly lost for words,' he teased. 'You'll lay one on me, perhaps?'

'I will.' Danni's breath was caught in her throat.

'Is that a threat or a promise? I trust you mean you'll lay a kiss on my lips.' He stepped nearer.

'Kiss nothing!' Danni exclaimed, feeling like a mouse being tormented by a cat. 'I think you'd better get out of here before I scream the place down.'

'Start screaming,' he laughed deep in his chest as his arms came around her in tight bands.

Danni tried to free her hands, wating to put some distance between them, his closeness eroding her defences. But his arms held her captive. She turned her lips from his kiss, only to have him tease her earlobe, so that not only did she have him to fight but her already surrendering defences.

'Will you please let me go? I have no desire whatsoever to have you kiss me!'

'It's a wife's duty to kiss her husband.' His voice was all teasing arrogance.

'I don't want to be your wife. I ... I want a divorce.'

'Well, I don't!' He still held her in his arms, but his eyes held a wary expression.

'And I know very well why you don't, too,' Danni burst out.

'Quite the little know-all, aren't you? No doubt you're going to fill me in.'

'I don't want to stay married to someone who married me to set a few suspicious minds at rest. No one would think I'd marry you if you'd had anything to do with Rick's death. What I don't understand is why you didn't simply publicise that home movie that Chris Damien supposedly has. It would have been less trouble,' Danni finished, near to tears.

Shiloh shook his head. 'For an intelligent girl you are incredibly dumb. How many times do I have to tell you I don't care what people think, I only care about what I believe of myself. And what you think of me.' He kissed her quickly on the lips. 'Do I have to spell it out? I married you because I loved you and I don't want to live without you. Now, prove it!' He relaxed his grip on her, taking her by surprise, so that she stood in the circle of his arms.

'Prove what?' Danni stammered.

'That you have no desire. Prove it by kissing me dispassionately,' said Shiloh, looking down at her through half closed eyes.

Danni could only look at him and he smiled crookedly before he lowered his head and his lips claimed hers, moving sensually, breaking down her resistance and fanning the spark of response that began as a flutter in the pit of her stomach and rose, threatening to have her lose her head completely. Her lips moved tentatively beneath his and reading her response his lips teased hers, parting her lips, probing and demanding.

Danni's head began to spin. How she wanted to believe what he said! If only she could forget . . . She had to break away now or she wouldn't have the strength or desire to carry it out. Summoning her reserves, she went to straighten her arms, thrust him away, but he had read her mind as usual.

The bed behind the back of her knees upset her balance and she collapsed on to the soft mattress gasping in shock. Shiloh's body was beside hers, his legs across hers, his hard maleness searing through the thin material of her skirt and blouse.

His hand was now free to caress her and her body responded of its own volition. And suddenly she knew she didn't want to fight him, this was where she wanted him. She needed him, and only that had any importance. The rest meant nothing. Motor racing. Marla. There was only this unity, his hands playing over the soft skin of her midriff, over the lacy covering of her bra to her breasts, and she murmured beneath his lips. She loved him so much.

'Seems to me this is where we came in,' he whispered as his fingers fumbled with the buttons on her blouse. 'Why do women wear so many clothes?' he muttered hoarsely.

Danni giggled and gave his shirt a tug, but it was caught fast in the belt of his jeans. 'I could say the same about men,' she said huskily.

They laughed together and he raised himself so that his shirt came loose in her hands. She moved her fingers over the firmness of his skin, and the smile died on her lips at the passion in his eyes. Sliding her hands under his shirt, she pulled him closer against her.

'God, Danni, if you only knew what you do to me!' he breathed against the hollow of her neck.

'Show me,' she whispered, and his lips claimed hers.

In the early hours of the morning Danni stirred sleepily, opening her eyes to find Shiloh looking down at her with a relaxed smile of satisfaction. The only light came from the living-room lamp which she had left burning.

She smiled and stretched languidly.

'You look as if you've lost twenty cents and found two dollars, Mrs O'Rourke,' he said happily.

She ran her hand lightly over his shoulder and her smile faded a little. 'I love you, Shiloh,' she said simply. 'I have almost from the first.'

'That goes for me, too, Danni.' He caught her hand and pressed his lips to her palm. 'Plain and simple, with no ulterior motives.'

'I was so mixed up about everything—the race, Rick,' Danni paused. 'I didn't want to believe you were responsible, but . . .'

'I know. I guess my attitude didn't help.' He sighed. 'I felt so bad about Rick it ate away at me all those months I was laid up. It was part of the reason I went back to racing, part guilt, and part conviction that I *had* lost my nerve. It was hinted to me so often I began to believe it.' He looked into her eyes. 'I knew myself that the accident was none of my doing, but I was too pigheaded to defend myself. I couldn't see why I had to prove it to the world that I was innocent. It was a ghost I had to lay, I have laid.

'Chris Damien understood why I needed to race again and he helped me convince the officials. He's quite a friend.' He was silent for a moment, his hand absently rubbing her bare shoulder. 'I used to think motor racing was my life, but last week, watching you on the track, I couldn't take it, Danni. It wasn't just because of your father's feelings that I was so angry. If anything had happened to you I'd have gone quietly insane.' He kissed her nose. 'I started thinking that if you felt half as bad about me while I was out on the track then—well, I guess motor racing lost some of its appeal for me.'

'Oh, Shiloh!' Danni put her lips softly to his chin.

'Danni,' he took her face in his hands, 'you and I, we can make a go of it. I'm not saying it will all be smooth sailing, we're both too volatile for that, but it could be the best.'

'The very best,' she smiled.

He pulled her into his arms, settling her head on his shoulder, and sighed peacefully. 'I wonder if an unemployed ex-racing driver will look as attractive to Marla Damien,' he asked seriously.

Danni struggled up to look at his face, seeing the twinkle of amusement in his eyes. 'I'm beginning to suspect you're quite vain, Shiloh O'Rourke ...' she said with mock exasperation.

'About Marla. I knew her before she married Chris. It didn't take me long to realise she was an empty package in pretty wrapping, and after the accident when she found other diversions I was considerably relieved,' he grinned. 'That little scene you inadvertently witnessed, the running was all Marla's, believe me. Besides being blind to any female but you, I wouldn't do that to Chris, no matter what. I owe him more than that.'

His grin left his face. 'Before I could reach you to explain you were out on the track. God, if anything had happened to you I wouldn't have forgiven myself! And I'd have slowly throttled the life out of Marla.'

'She did fancy you, you know.' Her fingers wove patterns in the mat of curling fair hair on his chest.

He laughed. 'Me and everyone even slightly well known. Marla likes to be the centre of attention.'

'I saw your photo, dining together. It was in the Sydney paper.' Danni watched his face.

He grimaced. 'I only went because Chris asked me to go. He was there as well. We were discussing my joining his racing team. He'd gone to take a phone call when that wretched photographer turned up. A very boring evening it was, too. I kept comparing all the girls with you, and none of them came close.'

'I'll give you a lifetime to keep telling me that,' Danni laughed.

'That's a promise I won't have any trouble keeping, Danni.' He was serious again. 'About your racing, I had no right to place that kind of stipulation on you. I don't want you to give up the Driver to Europe Competition unless you're absolutely certain you want to. You are ahead on points and I don't want you to feel . . .'

She put her finger over his lips. 'I'm more than sure. I want to retire. The series somehow lost its appeal when you came on the scene. And it isn't a feeling that happened at Oran Park last week. It was right from that moment you walked on to the practice track at Mallaroo. That's when it began. Besides,' a dimple appeared at the corner of her mouth, 'I can't see a barefoot and pregnant lady, no matter how liberated she is, being allowed to hare around the racing circuits in Europe, can you?'

'If you took it into your head to do it, I've no doubt you would,' Shiloh chuckled. 'While I turned white-haired, of course.' He kissed her soundly and their desire rose again.

'Shiloh, I have to go to work in a couple of hours,' Danni murmured.

'Ah, yes. Well, you'll have to have the day off. Your husband needs you,' he said in a lordly tone, and then looked down at her seriously. 'You don't have to continue working unless you want to. My father has been pressuring me to come into the family business, as you know, and I think now the time has come to use the engineering qualifications I spent years acquiring.' He winked at her. 'Now I have a wife and family to support.'

'Family? Aren't you being a little premature?' Danni laughed delightedly, putting her lips to the firm line of his jaw.

'Just leave it all to me, Mrs O'Rourke. In fact, it might not be a bad idea if we began working on that project right away,' he said, lowering his lips to hers.

Masquerade
Historical Romances

Intrigue
excitement
romance

THE BLACK MARQUIS
by Margot Holland

After her father and betrothed are killed at the Battle of
Hastings, the lovely Saxon Lady Elfrida is left defenceless.
She journeys to the court at London – to find that King
William has bestowed her hand on the arrogant man
known as the Black Marquis. But the proud Elfrida is
not so easily won . . .

DEVIL'S KIN
by Anne Herries

Hester Stanley runs away to become mistress of a man she
hardly knows. Living in pre-Revolution Paris, she is
blissfully happy with Beau Vane – until doubts begin to
emerge . . . Why does Beau claim to be the Devil's brother?
And, above all, why will Beau not marry her?

Look out for these titles in your local paperback shop from
11th December 1981

FREE-an exclusive Anne Mather title, MELTING FIRE

At Mills & Boon we value very highly the opinion of our readers. What <u>you</u> tell us about what you like in romantic reading is important to us.

So if you will tell us which Mills & Boon romance you have most enjoyed reading lately, we will send you a copy of MELTING FIRE by Anne Mather – absolutely FREE.

There are no snags, no hidden charges. It's absolutely FREE.

Just send us your answer to our question, and help us to bring you the best in romantic reading.

CLAIM YOUR FREE BOOK NOW

Simply fill in details below, cut out and post to: Mills & Boon Reader Service. FREEPOST. P.O. Box 236, Croydon, Surrey CR9 9EL.

The Mills & Boon story I have most enjoyed during the past 6 months is:

TITLE _____

AUTHOR_____ BLOCK LETTERS, PLEASE

NAME (Mrs/Miss) _____ EP4

ADDRESS _____

_____

_____ POST CODE _____

Offer restricted to ONE Free Book a year per household. Applies only in U.K. and Eire.
CUT OUT AND POST TODAY – NO STAMP NEEDED

Mills & Boon
the rose of romance